T0365685

The House by the Side of the Road

The House by the Side of the Road

JEAN BREMER

ARCHWAY
PUBLISHING

Archway Publishing books may be ordered
through booksellers or by contacting:

Archway Publishing
1663 Liberty Drive
Bloomington, IN 47403
www.archwaypublishing.com
844-669-3957

ISBN: 978-1-6657-4611-3 (sc)
ISBN: 978-1-6657-4612-0 (e)

Library of Congress Control Number: 2023911557

Print information available on the last page.

Archway Publishing rev. date: 09/13/2023

Who would you be if you had a cheerleader? A protector? A mentor? A teacher? A friend. Go find them. Look ahead, not back, and go for it!

ACKNOWLEDGMENTS

Special thanks to the Ladies of the (Book) Club, who read my manuscript and offered invaluable feedback: Linda, Barb, Kathy, Sheron, Mary, Carol, Wendy, and Jan. Love you all.

AUTHOR'S NOTE

Chicago is an amazing city. It has the second-tallest building in the Western Hemisphere. It is the third largest city in the US. There are Bulls and Bears lurking everywhere, at Soldiers' Field, the Board of Trade, and city hall.

But everything has a flip side, and here is Chicago's: it's the place the US military sends its doctors for combat training. In 2020, there were 2.7 million people (about the population of Mississippi) living in Chicago, one of five of them in poverty.

People on the street are Midwestern polite, respectful, and helpful. While beauty and wealth abound on the Gold Coast, there are areas where poverty and gun battles are the norm. And those gun battles have begun to spread across the affluent as well as the impoverished neighborhoods.

CHAPTER 1

Johnathan Richards stood up from his business class seat and graciously offered to get the carry-on for the woman seated next to him. The woman stretched, smiled, and accepted his offer. The flight from LA to Chicago was a long one, even in business class, but just sitting next to this elegant man had made it interesting. He reminded her of Errol Flynn in his heyday. Did anyone besides her remember Errol Flynn? The tall, handsome man had been a source of great interest to the flight attendants, with his movie-star good looks. He spent most of the flight on his laptop, probably managing his mega-successful business enterprises, they imagined. He occasionally checked his watch or pulled out papers from his leather briefcase. He was the epitome of the American dream, exuding charm, and everyone who saw him hoped he'd grace them with his attention. A flight attendant brought Richards his cashmere coat and helped him into it. He deplaned, made his way through the crowded O'Hare terminal carrying his Brunello Cucinelli bag, and headed out to meet his ride, which turned out to be a Mercedes-Benz Maybach S 580. The car pulled away from the busy airport into the dark night, merging into rush hour traffic.

That evening, Johnathan was enjoying an excellent fillet at the Gold Coast Club, his go-to residence when visiting Chicago. The wine pairing was exquisite, and the service even better. He wouldn't stay anywhere else. At 8:00 p.m., he rose from his regular table, put on his coat, and headed out to the front entryway to await his scheduled driver, who arrived promptly at 8:05 p.m. The driver didn't speak while proceeding to the prearranged destination. Soft jazz permeated the soundproof interior of the Cadillac Escalade. Richards was deep in thought, anticipating the meeting ahead of him. He enjoyed these meetings.

The car approached a palatial home in Kenilworth, a suburb north of Chicago and one of the wealthiest in America. The driver proceeded through the gates and pulled under the portico, where Johnathan disembarked. The car pulled away.

No conversation, thought Richards. *Excellent driver.*

The door to the house opened, and he was greeted pleasantly by an employee of the household, a lovely Hispanic woman.

"Good evening, Ida," Johnathan said as she took his coat and scarf.

"Good evening, sir," she replied. They had met many times before.

Johnathan was led into a parlor where five exquisitely dressed and physically fit individuals awaited him. They exuded money.

"John! Great to see you," the gentleman at the head of the table greeted him. Maxwell Randolph Menninger, a well-known philanthropist and industrialist with the pedigree of an American aristocrat, was their host tonight—a Harvard grad, sixth generation. Randolph Street in downtown Chicago had been named for one of his ancestors. He was the real deal.

The others followed Max's enthusiastic greeting as they arose and approached Johnathan with extended hands. It had been three months since their last meeting.

Drinks were ordered and places assumed. Attendees smiled and interacted like old friends, updating one another on golf triumphs, recent cruises, and family milestones. Once settled with cocktails in front of them, the time had come to briefly conduct business.

Brian Groen, a Northwestern alum in economics with a Wharton MBA and a key portfolio manager for a leading investment firm in the city, was the *money guy* for the partnership and had the full confidence of the group.

"We understand things are all set to move our product into place," Brian said. "What do you expect the delivery date and distribution timeline to look like, Johnathan? Our investors are looking forward to their return by the end of the quarter, as you know."

"Indeed," Johnathan affirmed. "I am very confident that this delivery will move smoothly and without incident."

"Excellent, Johnathan! It is always a great pleasure to work with you. Such a seamless operation and always a great return on investment. We will check back in at our next meeting in March. I would be happy to host as usual," said Randolph. Clearly this was not the first collaboration between this group and Johnathan.

"If there are no further questions for Johnathan, let's move into the solarium for cigars. We have so much more to catch up on!"

As the group picked up the conversation among themselves, they moved into the large solarium, where tropical plants, fountains, and pools of koi gave the feel of being in the Caribbean rather than a northern suburb of Chicago in the dead of winter.

CHAPTER 2

It was a dark and gloomy Friday evening as Helen Wagers headed out of her office building to her car. The weather was not supposed to improve, and while it may not have been prudent to strike out on a wild goose chase in it, she had one more loose end to tie up before she could call it a week.

The air was cold and whipped around the precipitation that hadn't yet decided whether to be rain, sleet, or snow. It being Chicago, it was possible to have all three within the same hour. The sky was steely gray and hung like a heavy pall over those brave individuals who found themselves hurrying to their next place of shelter, whether that be an El train, a subway, a building, a car, or a restaurant.

As she got to her battered old car, a green 2001 Honda Civic, she greeted it by name. They had been through many adventures over the years.

"Thank you for waiting for me, Edith! I know this weather is tough on your old bones."

Helen had decided that she and Edith would continue their adventures together if Edith was able. Edith had some job security in that Helen barely covered her rent on her caseworker salary, much less a new car.

It may be a long shot, but I need to try this lead to see if I can find Marty, she thought. *Such a good kid with so much baggage.* He'd failed to return to his group home all week, and more baggage was going to accumulate if he didn't check in by the end of today, which was basically now.

I can't believe he would do this. Things were going so well. I could tell it wasn't easy for him, but he was toughing it out, she thought.

Marty had reportedly taken a train out from downtown to the far south suburbs of the city and beyond. The terminus for the train was a park and ride in the middle of nowhere. She was familiar with it, having driven by it many times on her way to and from the school she attended in Central Illinois. It was primarily used by travelers coming from "downstate," the area south of the Chicago metropolitan area, which was most of the state of Illinois. Those who were uncomfortable driving in the city or didn't want to pay exorbitant fees to park for a few hours could leave their cars in the lot and board a train into the heart of downtown Chicago.

This house Marty went looking for either has to be walking distance from the parking lot of this park and ride, or he would have needed some other form of transportation, Helen thought. *This isn't walking weather.*

Snow had begun to fall as Helen exited I57 for I80. "Shit!" she said. And then through the gloom and falling snow, she spotted a ramshackle old house, no lights, boarded up, off to the side of the highway.

Well, there's a house, but it's abandoned, she thought. She'd keep an eye out for others.

Taking the exit from the highway toward the commuter parking lot, Helen found herself on a well-lit road in good condition. Continuing past the lot, trying to find the house she'd seen, the asphalt ended, and the road became gravel. Each side of the road had a three-foot-wide ditch and lots of overgrowth. Fields, brown and overgrown, with a light layer of wet snow bordered the road on each side. She was basically in a rural area at this point, although only a few miles from the highway.

Bleak, she thought.

As Helen turned on Edith's high beams to see if there were any other houses in range, the ground looked as though it had once been part of a farm.

Abandoned dirt, she thought. *Depressing.*

To stem the despair she felt, Helen made some noises that were supposed to sound like scary music, and then, speaking in her best Vincent Price voice, she articulated the scene as she was experiencing it.

"As darkness descended on the abandoned ground, a tired, sad, old house came into view. They were obvious companions, the ground, the house. Time passed and left them here together. Gray. Leached of all life and vitality.

"Good, eh, Edith? All that's missing is Michael Jackson."

If there is a house out here somewhere, there must be an access road to get to it, she thought. *Or at least a trace of one.* A trace would not be easy to find in the light snow that now coated the ground, but she'd come this far.

Driving around in the snow and darkness for half an

hour, taking small gravel roads leading from the main road and then other dirt roads from those, she finally got within a hundred feet of the old house she'd seen from the highway. At this point, it was the only house she'd come across. She thought she'd take a closer look, just in case there were squatters who'd seen Marty. Or worse, to see if Marty had made it this far, found nothing, and couldn't get back to the train in this weather.

She turned on her flashlight app, put on her coat, hat, and gloves, and called her bestie, Lilly. She and Lilly always talked to each other when they were walking from their cars to their apartments through dark streets at night. It was their attempt at safety in an unsafe world. She was going to have to be a little vague with Lilly this time though. Lilly would not be amused to learn that she was walking on an overgrown path toward an abandoned house in the dark … alone.

"Hi, Lilly. Can you talk for a couple minutes? I'm out of the city, so don't worry, but I'm alone, looking for a client."

"What?" was the response. "Are you crazy? It's dark. Give it up and go home. Get a police dog! Get another job!" Lilly was an accountant, obviously.

"So how was your day? Are you home from work? Have plans tonight? The weather looks lousy. You might want to stay in and catch the latest Kardashian episode," replied Helen.

I'm going to need to find a calmer safety buddy to call when necessary, Helen thought. *I'm afraid I'm going to give Lilly a heart attack.*

"Don't change the subject. Where's Ryan? I thought you were meeting up with him tonight," Lilly said.

When she was finished for the day, after this experience, she thought a warm bath and a glass of wine at her apartment sounded much better than an inebriated Ryan and his buddies.

"Um, they're at Embellish," Helen replied. "I'm meeting them there when I finish here. This shouldn't take long."

It is fair to say at this point that this is a little nutty, even for me, Helen thought.

Helen was known for her fearlessness and her sense of adventure. What petite coed chooses social work for a major and then becomes a caseworker for formerly incarcerated young adults, specializing in those who are bridging the juvenile/adult age range while incarcerated? Well, as her friends always answered, "Helen does, of course." But this was almost recklessness, and she would have given it up if she had not spent the past two hours looking for Marty, knowing he would blow his graduation date from supervision if she didn't talk to him today somehow—and if she hadn't needed an excuse to delay meeting Ryan.

All the while thinking of plan B in case this adventure became threatening, Helen continued to chat with Lilly, creeping steadily toward the spooky house, her cell phone flashlight on the ground to avoid detection if there happened to be anyone around.

"I just looked at my tracking app. What are you doing on the side of a highway so far from home? I can't believe you. You had better call me the minute you get safely back to your car. I should call Ryan," Lilly said.

It was time to get off the phone before Lilly completely freaked out. Helen said, "I'm fine, Lill. I'll call when I start home. The wind is making too much noise, and I can't hear you."

As she disconnected from the call, the wind whipped through the trees, and cars and trucks raced by on the highway, covering any noise she was making.

All I have to do now is quietly creep up to the house, peek inside to get a closer look, and then head back to the car, without being eaten by a wolf or a werewolf. Ha, not funny, she thought.

She approached the front of the house, thinking of every scary movie she'd ever seen, simultaneously.

"What the hayell am I doing?" she said, although there was so much noise around her that she alone knew she had spoken out loud. There was litter everywhere, blown from the highway, and a layer of dirt covered the porch. The stairs and the porch were rotten, and the windows boarded. She walked around the house, trying to see if there was a way to get inside. She was glad she had worn her heavy boots. This was no walk on the red carpet—fallen limbs, garbage, boards with nails sticking out, holes in the ground in unsuspected places. It was a minefield.

It's time to get out of this place and back to civilization, she thought. Once around the house, she hopscotched her way up the stairs, avoiding the holes. Reaching through the boards, she pushed lightly on the once elegant front door.

To her great surprise and maybe dismay, the door moved. Through a crack, Helen saw light inside the house and smelled something good. She called in to draw attention from the inhabitants, if they were alive and human, but her voice was overpowered by the noise from the cars and wind. She'd come this far undetected; maybe she could get in undetected and see what was happening and who was there. Or maybe she should run like hell. She was aware of the risk she was taking and thought, *Sorry for the wasted college tuition, Mom and Dad.*

Ducking in under the plywood that crisscrossed the front door, she found herself standing in a beautiful, warm hallway with a small but elegant fountain. She could hear lively conversation in the next room. She smelled roasted coffee and baked dessert and again marveled at how beautiful and warm it was in there.

While she should have felt threatened and afraid, she was at ease and could see, down a hallway in front of her, a classically decorated living room. She crept up to the pocket doors past a broad stairway and saw an empty room with a roaring fire. It looked like a Hallmark movie set.

Backtracking to the front hallway, she followed voices coming from the room to her left, the dining room, she guessed, where vampires were most likely sharing a gourmet meal. She took consolation in the knowledge that vampires didn't eat real food, which was definitely what she was smelling. Of course, she debated, that was either a good sign or a bad sign, since that would mean the only food they'd have would be her.

She crept up to the pocket doors that were partially open and quietly said, "Hello?" She knew she should feel intense fear at this moment and was aware that she did not, which she found to be strange. In fact, she felt wonder.

People were sitting around a table, all engaged in a variety of lively conversations. All looked healthy, clean, and cheerful. Helen cleared her throat. "Um, excuse me. I apologize for letting myself in," she said. "I'm actually looking for someone, Marty Mun—"

"Hi, Helen. Right here! Come in and warm up. It's cold out there."

It was Marty. But he was almost unrecognizable. His voice was strong, and his skin looked healthy. He seemed to be approaching a normal weight, and most astonishing of all, he was smiling.

"Sorry if I've worried you. I'm good! Sit down! Join us! Have something to eat. Meet my friends. Please," Marty said.

CHAPTER 3

When Marty was six, he started school, which didn't go too well for him. Spanish was spoken in his home by his grandparents, who raised him. He fell behind in reading and never caught up. As he progressed through the grades, his reading improved, but he was so far behind he could never catch up on the content he'd missed in the preceding grades. Consequently, he ended up in remedial everything, with the so-called bad kids and dumb kids, and he took on that identity along with them.

His greatest joy was to duck into the church located between his grandparents' apartment and his school. There was always music coming from the church. If no one was around but the pastor, he'd let Marty play the piano. If the choir or church musicians were practicing, Marty just sat and listened. When the pastor heard Marty playing around on the piano one day, he realized that Marty was playing what he'd heard by ear. He could replicate any song the choir did, from memory. And he could improvise and create beautiful music that seemed to emanate from his soul.

The pastor and the church became his refuge. He began accompanying the choir and playing before services.

When his grandfather died, his grandmother moved, and even the music was gone. He knew no one in his new school, except the kids in his classes, who were often truant. When his grandmother died, he joined the truant kids. He quit going to school, was arrested, spent time in juvenile detention, was put back out on the street on probation, and got in trouble again, following his friends into gangs. He was a nice kid, a very talented kid, but once the gang money and access to drugs got hold of him, none of that mattered anymore.

And as a result, he ended up under Helen's supervision. This was his second supervisory period. He had gone through detention, supervision, release, back in with the gang, detention, and now supervision again. He was about to be released, and Helen was concerned. She didn't want to see the cycle repeated. His next offense would be tried in adult court, and he'd end up in adult jail. He would enter a whole different league.

CHAPTER 4

Accepting the chair offered to her, Helen sat down at the table. An attractive, even beautiful woman, who might have been mid-fifties or maybe older, jumped up to get a cup of coffee and a plate of pastries for Helen. The others all began praising the baking skills of the woman, whose name was Frances. She was apparently the best baker in the world, or close to it if they were to be believed.

Frances returned to the table with a beautiful china cup filled with coffee, along with several small fruit pies. Her hands were elegant, and her movements graceful.

"Here, dear. Warm up. We've finished dinner, but I can fix you something if you'd rather have a meal than a pastry," Frances said, placing a beautiful linen napkin in front of Helen.

"Thank you so much, but I'm fine. I don't want to interrupt your meal." Saying this, she realized she was famished and took a piece of the cherry pie off her plate. It was, it turned out, the best cherry pie she'd ever tasted—and maybe that had ever been made in the world, as had been foretold. Who were these people?

Those around the table allowed Frances to lead the conversation with the new guest. It was clear she was the hostess. After niceties about the weather, the conversation became more in depth.

Was the traffic heavy? And the weather, had it turned yet? What was Helen's job exactly? And for whom did she work? How long ago had she graduated from college? Which college had she attended? How did she choose social work? What did she think of her client load? Was it too much to handle? And what was her impression of those who led the city's services (from her fresh perspective)? In other words, highly intelligent conversation with highly intelligent people, some of whom had dealt firsthand with the city programs and services they were discussing.

"Enough about me," Helen said. "I'd love to know more about all of you."

The hostess, the elegant woman, was Frances Miller. At the opposite end of the table was Donald Fernandez, an older gentleman, meticulously groomed and with beautiful diction. To Frances's right was Emma Wright, a young woman in her late teens, with beautiful green eyes and rich brown hair. Next to Emma sat a striking young African American man who introduced himself as Zachary Birmingham.

To Frances's left sat Marty. And next to Marty was Angela McCall, another young woman, perhaps a couple years older than Emma. She had lovely Irish freckles, strawberry-blond hair, and striking blue eyes.

The whole group struck Helen as one of the most refined and varied she had ever had the pleasure of joining for coffee. The conversation was lively and informed, intelligent, and challenging. In general, she was dumbfounded. What was happening here? In this place, Marty was clearly a completely different person than she had known—clean, clear eyed, sharp minded, and, most of all, confident. She had to know more about this place and these people, if for no other reason than to understand what was happening to her client Marty.

Helen looked back to Frances, complimenting her on her hospitality and asking her if her mother had been a society hostess, or had she perhaps attended a finishing school?

"I did have a very privileged upbringing," Frances acknowledged. "In fact, this house and land has belonged to my family for a hundred and fifty years. When my father died, I was the only living heir, and it was left to me. In my grief, I lost my way for a while, and my life was not centered here. The house was left empty and fell into disrepair."

"Oh, I'm so sorry," Helen said.

"It was a long time ago now, dear. I was only a girl. Life goes on."

"Perhaps we could move into the living room, Frances?" said Mr. Fernandez. "I don't believe you've ever shared the story of your youth with the full group. Would you be willing to do that for us? It might be helpful to some in the room."

Once settled in the overstuffed furniture in the spacious living room, with the fireplace crackling and the smell of burning logs filling the room, Frances sat down with a cup of tea. She began to talk about herself in a way that seemed like she was talking about someone else.

"A little girl was born to two loving parents. She had one sibling. They were happy, healthy, and privileged. Her mother was involved with the community and supported her father's career. She ensured that her children had training in the arts, sports, and languages—culture basically. The family traveled extensively and had friends in many places," she said, smiling at Donald.

"The young woman was relatively tall for her age, five eight, and by all accounts, she would grow to be a great beauty. Her grades were excellent, and she excelled at music, math, and drama."

"The world was her oyster," Frances reminisced.

"She started at a private prep school when she turned fourteen. It was at that time that the road took a sharp and unexpected turn."

Frances continued, "Toward the end of her freshman year in school, the girl's mother was diagnosed with, and quickly succumbed to, colon cancer. The following year, her sibling, a sister two years her junior named Rose, was diagnosed with leukemia, which claimed her life by the time Frances was sixteen.

"After this, her father began to experience depression, quit talking, and withdrew even further into the shell where he'd spent the past two years. The young woman was sent to boarding school out east to finish high school. During her senior year of high school, she was called to the administrator's office and told that her father had taken his own life. According to his will, his estate was in trust for her. She was an heiress with absolutely no one left in the world.

"Her journey after that was bumpy at best, defined by greedy relatives, preying suitors, and eventually prescription drugs and alcohol. Plagued by hepatitis C and a monkey she couldn't seem to shake, she ended up with the same depression that had taken her father. She wandered the streets, sleeping under bridges, eating at rescue missions. The drugs caused her to run afoul of the law on several occasions. Life on the street was often violent, and she ended up hospitalized several times. All alone. No visitors. No family. Alone."

Frances suggested that she had become well known in the social services office thirty-five years ago. Her file would most likely read like a tragic novel of lost potential.

"But that was long ago," Frances uttered softly. "And the beauty has returned. Thankfully."

As Frances talked, the others listened in supportive silence, occasionally intoning sympathetically. Helen listened too, as she had been taught to do at social work school, but her mind couldn't help racing around the stories of Marty and Frances. How differently they had been raised, yet their stories were tragically similar, those of lonely and sad children left on their own to negotiate the world. And yet, with such gifts, such natural talents they had never been able to deliver to the world around them, because no one had nurtured them.

●⁖·⁖

Marty sat down at the piano and began to play softly. The music changed the mood in the room, and it began to lighten. Marty improvised, and a beautiful tune flowed from the piano. This was the first time Helen had heard him play. She was mesmerized. The others got up and began to dance and clap, and the mood was as happy as it had been sad just fifteen minutes earlier.

Afterward, Frances read the most beautiful poetry Helen had ever heard, only to learn that it was original and composed by Zachary, the African American Adonis she'd met at the dinner table.

Helen suddenly became aware of the time; it was past 8:00 p.m., and she hadn't talked to Marty about missing his check-in with her this week. She politely excused herself to her hosts and asked to speak privately with Marty. They walked into the front hallway where Helen had originally entered the house.

"Marty, I could report you for violating the terms of your probation. You are supposed to be working and checking in with me every Monday," she began. "It's Friday. I'm glad I found you.

"You seem to be doing well here and have aligned yourself with some wonderful people. I don't want to interfere with the progress you're making, but I must know that I can reach you and that you will be checking in with me on a regular basis."

"I apologize, Helen. I was in a bad place when we met the week before last. I was afraid I was going to go backward like I did last time I was released. And then I met Frances online. She invited me to join what she called a support group, where I could also stay. Since I'll need a place to stay after my supervision is up, I thought I'd check it out. I've been here ever since. I would like to terminate my job. Zach and I have been doing some composing, and we plan to market our work online.

"I haven't been tempted to use drugs, and I've never felt more at home or healthier than I have in this place. No one is asked to leave if they want to stay. There is enough room in the house for each of us to have our own sleeping room and space to pursue our interests. We eat together and share our day around the table. It's the closest thing I've ever had to a family, and I want to stay here."

"I get it," Helen replied. "I can see how well you're doing here. I won't report this breach for now, but you've got to promise to stay connected with me. I'll write up my report and report the change in employment and residence. And I'll drop in to see you again soon.

"You're so close to the end of your supervision period. Please, please, stick with it. I'd love to see you stay as happy and healthy as you are today … forever," said Helen, with emotion. "And I'll put in the paperwork to reassign you from your supervision living space to a permanent living space. Hopefully they will accept it a few weeks early."

Marty reached out and hugged her. He knew she was in his corner. He didn't want to disappoint her. He also wanted to honor his grandparents. They had sacrificed so much for him. He wanted to stay clean. He felt like he could this time, if he could stay in this place and with these people. For now, at least, until he was stronger.

CHAPTER 5

The glow of the environment she'd just left made the outside seem more foreboding than it had been when she arrived. She got into the car. "Hey, Edith, I'm back! And still alive!" she said. She quickly texted Lilly, with numerous spelling errors as her hands shivered. It was so cold.

She had to meet Ryan now, and she dreaded it. Ryan was her college boyfriend—her first boyfriend other than Matthew Lombard from fifth grade, who had pulled her hair and chased her in the schoolyard, which was how she knew he was her boyfriend.

She and Ryan had been together for three years, having met through a friend on her dorm floor who knew Ryan from classes they shared. The friend and Helen ran into him at a party, where she was introduced to him, and that was it. They had a lot in common. They both grew up in the Chicago suburbs, for one. They loved the outdoors and adventure. They loved to travel, see movies, run in 5Ks, then 10Ks, and ultimately the Chicago Marathon their first year out of college. A challenge that required courage and endurance was exciting to them both.

And they shared big dreams about their future. Ryan was going to make a fortune in his twenties, allowing them to continue their adventures without worrying about money. Helen was going to figure out how to help people realize their potential. She'd said to Ryan many times, "Can you imagine what the world would be if people lived up to their God-given potential?" They were going to live up to theirs and show others how to do it too.

In college, she was amazed to have found someone who had the same enthusiasm to experience things as she did, and yet it seemed that their interests had changed since they started their careers. She often had a tough time remembering what it was that had brought them together, because whatever it had been didn't seem to be keeping them together now that they were out in the world.

Ryan was at some downtown bar full of guys wearing ties, who were drinking shots, talking about trades and vast amounts of money they'd seen risked all day. Their whole focus was on money, making it and spending it.

Helen, conversely, found herself dealing with people who'd been dealt almost no cards in life. She found herself trying to find the *person* inside of her clients—that is, the one they had pushed deep down inside themselves in order to survive. There was almost nothing going on in her world that had to do with money, other than the lack of it. She made none, and her clients had none. It was gut-wrenching to see the circumstances people had survived, often at an incredibly young age. And it was inspiring too. Her clients were the opposite of the educated, ambitious, handsome, extravagant crowd Ryan associated with and wanted to emulate.

As she mulled over what to do next, she marveled at what she'd seen this evening. She'd seen a lot of unusual lifestyles in her line of work, but this was new. Today had not been a regular day. She needed to think. It was disorienting. How would she be able to express what she'd seen to her colleagues, much less to Ryan and his drinking friends? Because that house and the community it sheltered seemed outside of reality, while at the same time being the most real thing she'd seen in a long, long time.

Winding back through the overgrowth, she found her way back to the parking lot and then merged onto I80. She was stuck in traffic, which she shouldn't have been, given the hour. There must have been an accident. The sky was aglow with flashing red lights sparkling through a filter of light snow. The lights of emergency vehicles—vehicles there to rescue.

Rescue, she thought. *There's something about that.* Then she sat back, relaxed, and was thankful for the time she was being afforded to just be and feel. Perhaps she'd intuit something about the meaning of what she'd experienced tonight.

She texted Ryan, "Sorry to be late. On I80, far out in the burbs, stuck in traffic. Salt trucks everywhere. I'll keep you posted. Don't wait for me for dinner. Just let me know where you go, and I'll meet you if I can. Have fun!"

◦⸰∵

Traffic did not subside. Turning on the radio, she heard about the winter storm watch in the area. *Best to get home now while I still can*, she thought. Ah, perfect. Nature had smiled on her, or was abusing her, depending on one's perspective.

It snowed heavily overnight and continued through the weekend. As a result, she and Ryan were never able to get together. In fact, Ryan had crashed at one of his friend's on Friday night and didn't get home at all over the weekend. Helen could tell from his texts and their phone conversations that the party, which had started on Friday night, had continued all weekend.

All she could make of her experience on Friday was that she'd stepped into some parallel universe. The question was, what now? How did she document her visit with Marty? How could she require Marty to leave that house to appear in court and get his monthly blood tests? Would he be able to maintain his newfound peace and stability outside of the house?

And what had she witnessed? Who supported the household? She'd have to investigate that. How could the exterior of the house appear abandoned when the interior was light, cheerful, and as elegant as it had been when it was new a hundred years ago? And warm! And it must have had Wi-Fi if Marty initially interacted with Frances online. It had Wi-Fi?

So many questions. She'd need to go back again. Perhaps on Friday? In the meantime, she was happy for the snow. It gave her solitude and time to write up her case reports from the week—and to sleep. And to think.

CHAPTER 6

On Monday, Helen was able to get to work on the train but only just barely. At about 10:00 a.m., she stepped off the El and onto the platform. She descended the stairs and high-stepped through the snow toward her office building. There were piles of snow at every curb and corner, little mountains to climb over, and very little traffic. The snow had stopped during the night on Sunday, and for a moment in time, the city was clean, white, and quiet.

Hopefully people will stay home, she thought, although she was glad to be out. The security guy in the lobby didn't seem as happy as she felt about being at work. She avoided conversation with him. He was grumpy on a good day, and this, apparently, was not a day he would call good.

Once inside her office suite, she saw that the lights were on. There were others in the office—hopefully not many.

"Morning, Tom," she said as she passed her supervisor's office. Tom was forty-something, tall, gay, and charming. He and his husband, Robert, were the proud parents of two dogs and a cat, all of whom lived in greater comfort and elegance than she and her roommates.

"Morning, Helen," he said. "How was your commute? Most people couldn't make it into the city—or didn't try. Kevin's here too, of course. It would have been a good day to stay home."

"Yep," Helen replied, "but the snow kept me in all weekend, and I got caught up on my paperwork. I hope everyone stays home so I can accomplish something. Maybe some of my clients will be stuck somewhere and will answer their phones for a change.

"Besides," she continued, "I always think it's cool to be out on days when nature has taken over. The streets are deserted. The sounds are different. And I especially enjoy it when humanity must bow to a higher power. It puts us in our place."

"Agreed. Enough about philosophy though; what are we going to do for lunch?" he asked. "You know how I worry about my next meal at all times."

"Tom, this is Chicago. By noon, they'll be delivering pizza like it's the Fourth of July."

"Yep. You're right." He shrugged. "I should know better."

"How'd you get here?" she asked.

Tom reminded her that he and Robert lived in the South Loop. "I walked. Or more accurately, climbed snowdrifts.

"I have some research to do, and I'm hoping for some peace and quiet like you are. Our police liaison sent me a few emails over the weekend, saying there is talk on the street that something big is being planned. The gangs are agitated, as if they are getting ready for one of their professional events."

"Any clue what it's all about?" Helen asked.

"None. But the CPD has asked us to run it by our clients to see if they have any insight. They also warned that we may see some of our clients revert to the behaviors that got them onto our roles initially."

"Boy, I hate to hear that." Helen moaned. She was new enough to this work to have great hope for her charges, unlike Tom and others, who had more experience and knew it could sometimes take several rounds of arrest, jail, parole, and supervision to see if they'd ever be able to stay clean. And some never could.

"I know you're still idealistic. A bright-eyed, hopeful, save-the-world caseworker. I wish I still had that hope. Now I'm happy to see one in ten clients move into a more stable lifestyle. Even if they want to, their baggage holds them back."

At that point, Tom's phone began to ring, and he excused himself. Helen headed for the kitchen, hoping there was coffee made. There was not. She made a pot, poured a cup, and headed to her cubicle. She wanted to investigate a few things from last Friday.

CHAPTER 7

It was 9:00 a.m., and the house was coming to life. The world outside had literally turned into a winter wonderland. No more nasty pollution and dirt from the traffic but a soft and beautiful white cover, blanketing the tree limbs and the bushes. All the earth seemed to be still and quiet, with only the occasional plow and salt truck progressing slowly past on the highway.

The residents had gathered once again around the dining room table to enjoy coffee, bagels, and fruit, all prepared and set out by the beautiful and talented Frances. Every meal was like a royal banquet, without all the bowing of course, and the residents never tired of the beauty and creativity they found when they gathered to nourish their bodies and souls around this table.

Now that the roommates were beginning to use their talents to create, they were excited to see what each day would bring. After a quick breakfast and expression of gratitude to Frances, they headed to different parts of the house to work.

Zachary and Marty headed to the parlor. Although

Marty had only just arrived at the house, he and Zachary seemed like their talents were synergistic, like Rodgers and Hart, or Lennon and McCartney.

Marty was composing music on the piano, while Zachary drafted lyrics. Once finished, they would post the music on their new website, created by the wonderfully talented Angela. They had received a lot of positive feedback over the past week and were hopeful that something they had produced would reach those who purchased music for established artists to record.

In the meantime, they produced jingles for national products and sent them to ad reps for those products. In just the week since Marty had been there, they'd sold two jingles at $2,500 a pop. Marty had never made that amount of money in a day in his life—legally, that is.

Angela bid on IT jobs, helped Zachary and Marty record their music and post it, researched opportunities for Emma, and recorded auditions and soundtracks for her, submitting them in the appropriate format. She was having the time of her life.

Donald sat a bit longer at the table as the young people headed off to their respective areas of the house to work. He felt happy around Frances. They had known each other since childhood, when his father, a professor of languages like himself in Mexico, had worked with Frances's father to translate manuals for his business. The two families had become close, vacationing together and sharing holidays. She was beautiful, intelligent, talented, gracious, and everything else you'd say about the person you adored. He was smitten. No doubt. He always had been. The only time they had ever been out of touch was when Frances hit rock bottom after her family's implosion.

They talked about the day.

"What's on your agenda?" he asked.

"Well, meal planning for the week and the grocery order. Blog post and checking some sites for people who might round out our little family," Frances replied. "Hopefully they can deliver groceries to the parking lot, and I can meet them there; otherwise, we'll be scraping the bottom of the crisper drawer and making soup. This snow is going to slow things down today.

"You?" she asked.

"I'm doing more translating. These contracts with Frigidaire and Microsoft for instruction manuals are coming in fast and furiously," Donald replied. "I'll be in the library all day.

"What do you make of Marty's friend?" he asked, changing from small talk to big talk.

"The young woman, Helen, seemed very kind, and sincerely interested in getting Marty through this rough time and back onto his feet," replied Frances thoughtfully. "What was your impression?"

"I agree. It is a risk though, having someone on the outside aware of this place."

Frances shifted in her chair.

"It is. But was this place ever going to be able to remain completely invisible? There are the people who remodeled the interior and installed the HVAC—all the vendors, really.

I worked with them one at a time, so they never interacted with each other, but they are all out there somewhere, and they know about this place. I assume they think we abandoned the project, since the outside looks so forlorn. At least I hope they think that, but who knows? I knew the day would come, though I didn't know what it would look like, that we'd have to interact with the outside. And now we are on this path, and we must navigate.

"At this point, I think I'm more concerned about ways to keep Marty from going back out there. I'm not sure he can manage the world yet, and Helen says he'll need to appear in court eventually. That is going to require some thought and preparation," she said.

Sipping the last of their coffee, they parted, Frances to the kitchen and Donald gazing after her.

Beautiful music came from behind the twelve-foot pocket doors leading into the parlor as Donald walked past on his way to the library.

Zachary listened, then scribbled on a pad of paper, then listened, then scribbled. Occasionally he'd ask Marty to go back to the beginning, and he'd sing the lyrics he'd been developing along with the music.

This would sometimes lead to a finished product after an hour or two. Other times, they'd change the song from a ballad to a rock tempo or even take the refrain and develop it into a jingle, using various products as examples. Later, with Angie's help, they'd send out their work for consideration by possible customers.

When they got going, it was often noon before they realized they should break for something to eat and maybe go to the bathroom. This was one of those mornings. The snow outside gave the room, which was always quiet and insular, an even more soundproof feel—like a recording studio.

They had written an amazing song that was probably finished, but they'd let it lie and would go over it one more time later today to make sure. It was one of those tunes they imagined Carlos Santana would be great on with a young talent, much the way he had done with Rob Thomas and Michelle Branch. Angie would help them research whose hands it would need to get into to be heard and then get it into those hands, and they'd post it on their website of course.

"Any thoughts about Helen's visit yesterday, Marty? She seemed cool," commented Zachary.

"She is a very good person, Zach. I hope I haven't gotten her into trouble by missing my check-in last week," Marty answered sincerely. "I'm fortunate to have her for my caseworker. She really believes in her clients. I'd like to make her proud. Hell, I'd like to make *me* proud.

"I am concerned about the in-person check-in dates though," he continued. "My old gang would like nothing better than to get their hands on me, and they seem to have eyes everywhere in the city."

Zachary thought about it for a minute. "Maybe you could check in online?"

"Maybe," replied Marty, "but I still have to be drug tested on a regular basis. When I go to Stroger, where the city sends all clients, I know word will get out that I'm around again."

"Well, no one's going anywhere today, so let's not worry about it. Maybe Helen will figure it out." Zachary, who smelled something good coming from the dining room, said, "Let's go see what the goddess of gourmet has whipped up in her kitchen for lunch today."

CHAPTER 8

Johnathan Richards awoke in his beautiful salon room, turned on the TV, and looked out the window. This was not LA; of that, he was certain.

"Dammit," he said. It was Monday after the snowstorm. After the meeting with his investors, he needed to choose reliable contractors. Fortunately, he had the best organizer in the city, in any city he'd worked with—Joey Caruso. The day's meetings would be key to his plan and its timely implementation.

He purposely chose to have his meetings outside his club, although they had meeting space. He didn't want to be associated with anyone who might have a reputation or be recognizable. It would have been convenient today though, given the weather. He shouldn't have too much trouble getting to the Drake, since his club was relatively close, but he knew transportation would be a challenge for those he would be meeting with. It would be a good test of their tenacity, and he had learned not to underestimate Chicago. They would clear snow, and things would be up and running in a heartbeat. The bigger the challenge, the more the city took it on. But that was Chicago. Because of this, it was a most excellent place for his business endeavors.

He called his local organizer to check on the schedule for the day.

"Joey. Johnathan. Weather sucks. What's the plan for our ten o'clock, two o'clock, and four o'clock meetings? I have a flight back to the coast tonight."

"Yeah, John," replied Joey in his thick Chicago accent. "I got things lined up—a meeting room at the Drake. Catered lunch. Several guys from different, um, distributor groups, lined up to consider partnership from south, west and north sides. We will have a solid plan by the end of the day."

"Great. Later," said Johnathan. He had to admit the plan was perfect. He'd be able to cab it over to the Drake Hotel, taking his bag with him, and leave for the airport after the four o'clock meeting. By that time, the streets and highways would be perfect, and he'd make his flight with no problem.

CHAPTER 9

After breakfast, Emma and Angela, the two young women at the house, went to the living room, where Angela's desk and equipment were set up, to work on leads for Emma. Those leads might be opportunities for commercials, acting parts, or voiceovers. Angela had the research skills to find the leads online and the technical skills to record Emma's demos. Angela was Emma's biggest fan. She could see the range of her talent from the variety of auditions and demos she had recorded for her.

The two young women had met when they worked together at Subway, when Angela was at community college working on a certificate in information management and technology. They had enjoyed working together there and had become very close since finding and taking refuge at the house. They had become like sisters, something Angela had a lot of and had missed desperately since taking refuge at the house for safety. When she wasn't helping Emma, Angela did online coding on a freelance basis and was making a very good income doing it. And she helped the others in the house with their IT needs of course.

Emma felt good about the work she and Angela had completed that morning. She felt good about so many things since moving to the house. She was grateful to be there. They, too, headed to the dining room for lunch.

Emma had come to the house first, when only Zachary lived there with Frances and Donald. She had connected with Frances online and then brought Angela to meet with Frances shortly afterward.

Emma had been looking for an affordable studio apartment outside the city when she found a blog titled "Finding the Perfect Nest." The host of the blog offered to share a lead with her on Messenger. That person was Frances. The place she described was outside the city. It was a house, and she'd have a room and bathroom of her own. Meals were provided if the tenant wished. No rent amount was specified. She'd need to pursue the lead for more information, according to Frances.

Emma scheduled a time to see the unit the next day. She had to work in the evening but could get out south to see the place in the afternoon.

The next morning, she took the train out south of the city to University Park, where there was a big parking lot in the middle of nowhere. This was almost the end of the line for the train, which serviced downstate travelers who either didn't want to drive in Chicago traffic or didn't want to pay exorbitant fees to park their car while in the city. Or both.

I hope I got this right, she thought.

Just then, a large black truck pulled up. A beautiful

woman, who looked like she was in her fifties, with graying hair, put down her window and addressed her politely. "Excuse me, dear, but are you Emma?"

"I am," said Emma.

"I'm here to take you to the house. I'm Frances. We communicated online yesterday. The others are excited to meet you."

The others? thought Emma. *Tenants? Yes, I guess that makes sense. I should be able to get a good impression of the place by meeting other people who live there and hearing what they say about the place.*

Frances had a lovely demeanor, which, Emma reminded herself, didn't mean she wasn't an ax murderer. But Emma felt calm rather than suspicious around this woman. She'd have to admit that there were moments when her mind sent up flares, but her gut stayed calm. Frances had that effect on people.

One of those flares went up when Frances left the paved road from the parking lot and started down a gravel road into the country. Flare number two happened when Frances turned off that road onto an overgrown, barely detectable, dirt drive that led to a boarded-up, abandoned farmhouse. And then there was flare three, when she drove around the back of the house and directly into a barn that was in about the same shape as the house and the rest of the property. Frances jumped out of the truck, opened the back door, and grabbed two bags of groceries.

"Can I help you carry those?" Emma found herself asking. "And are we, um, going far?"

"No, dear," Frances answered. "We're here," she said as

she headed up the back stairs, skillfully avoiding holes in the steps. "Watch yourself on the stairs."

And I was worried about living in a dump in the city! Emma thought.

Once on the porch, Emma saw a weathered door with gray wood planks nailed in a crisscross pattern, presumably to block anyone from entering, and yet with a slight nudge from Frances, it had swung open. As Emma followed Frances, she thought of Dorothy stepping out of her house and into Oz. They entered a beautiful kitchen with state-of-the-art commercial appliances, decorated in a French country style and smelling really, really good.

"Pardon me, dear," said Frances, "while I put away the groceries. Go right through this door into the dining room, and you'll see the foyer directly beyond. There's a coat tree in the front hallway. There is also a powder room if you need to freshen up.

"Lunch will be ready in an hour, so if you don't mind, I'd like a couple of my friends to host you while I throw something together. You'll find them in the living room, which you'll see from the foyer, straight back from the fountain. I'm sure one of them will come out to greet you. They are good people, like you, dear, and they're very excited to meet you. I assume you have questions and would like to see the house. They can show you around while I get things ready."

She hung her coat on the rack in the foyer where there were other coats, stepped quickly into the powder room, put 911 into her phone, just in case she needed to hit *send*, and looked at herself in the mirror.

What she saw was a petite brunette with striking green eyes and an oval face. Her niceness came across in her visage, as did the force of her personality. She had confidence and a strong sense of who she was. And she was excellent at reading people. So much so that she was able to quickly sum up those she met and characterize them in her acting, making her an amazing actor.

She didn't want to take on a character this time though, which is where she always went to be safe. She wanted to be her authentic self. She wanted to find a place where she was truly safe this time. And if this place wasn't it—and this was a very strange place, so she knew not to get her hopes up—she'd keep looking. Or at least she'd find a place of her own where she could take care of herself. She'd had enough of the unstable life. She was ready for some peace.

A striking young man, with rich, dark skin and looking like he could be a model for *Ebony* magazine, stepped out of what she imagined was the living room and stuck out his hand, saying, "Emma, I presume? My name is Zachary. I live here at the house. We are so excited to make your acquaintance." His voice was smooth and soothing. It was unique. He was unique.

"Hello," she said. "Pleased to meet you, Zachary. I'm happy to be here."

"Well, you'll be even happier when lunch is served," he said, which made her wonder if they were having fried rat or some other bizarre fare, bursting the bubble she seemed to be in. It sure didn't smell like fried rat coming from that kitchen though.

I have no idea what fried rat smells like, although anything but Subway sounds good, she thought, regretting ever having watched *Whatever Happened to Baby Jane*.

She followed Zachary into a beautiful room. The furnishings were classically beautiful, like the movie set of a stately home. The fireplace surround was made of green marble, and the curtains were velvet. The furniture was overstuffed, with a traditional floral pattern, and the side tables had marble tops on an ornately carved base. A classic oriental rug pulled it all together.

An older gentleman, tall and slender, wearing a tweed jacket and with an ascot tied around his neck, sat in a wing chair to the right of the fireplace. He stood to introduce himself as they entered the room.

"Emma, we are so pleased to have you visit today. My name is Donald. I am a resident here at the house. Zachary and I would like to answer any questions you may have about living here and show you the house. Please sit with us for a bit so we can become acquainted."

He gestured toward a chair directly across from the fireplace and took his seat. Zachary sat down on the settee to his right. They gave her some space, which she appreciated.

"Let us begin with introductions. I am Professor Donald Fernandez. I am originally from Mexico City, where I was on the faculty at the university there. I was educated in the US and have been back here for quite a few years now. I have resided at the house since Frances began renovations."

Zachary Birmingham explained a bit about himself. "I am a California native," he said. "I am a writer. I have done movie scripts, written poetry, and collaborated with songwriters to develop lyrics. I have been at the house for three years."

"And we understand that you are an actress. Can you share a bit about your experience in theatre?" Donald asked.

"I was born and raised in Florida," Emma began. "I had acted in community theatre, commercials, and in high school productions. I had dreamed of going to New York after high school to do stage work.

"Growing up, my parents had professional jobs, often traveling for their respective jobs. My brother and I were raised by nannies, with no expense spared for lessons, camps, coaches—whatever activities we wanted. Money was never an issue with them; time was.

"I was, of course, expected to go to a prestigious university and *become* something," she said. "A doctor, lawyer, professor, business executive, whatever. It didn't matter. As you might imagine, the idea of going to New York to try to make it on Broadway was not what they had in mind. If I pursued that, I would be on my own. No negotiating.

"I was a strong-willed teenager who bristled at being told what to do by these parents who were pretty much absent my whole life, or at least that's the way I looked at it then. And I guess I still do now," Emma mused, looking up at the ornate crown molding. This room reminded her of a theatre. This whole house did.

While talking, she had the fleeting thought that Donald and Zachary listened more attentively to her than her parents had ever done.

"And considering how many young people strike out on

their own to make it on Broadway, I had considerable success from the very beginning," Emma remarked, somewhat incredulously. "I was young and could sing, dance, and act.

"What I didn't have was enough money to live on. I ended up working minimum-wage jobs that took all my time, so I couldn't get to auditions. When I did make an audition, I wasn't properly dressed and smelled like fried chicken or whatever fast-food job I'd just come from. I didn't have the support I needed to make it. I came to Chicago thinking I might have a chance in this theatre community, figuring the cost of living would be somewhat more affordable than New York. But I'm back in the cycle of working two jobs, without benefits, without time to audition, and barely making enough money to live on. I was hoping this place would be affordable for me since I'd only be renting one room."

"Well, we are certainly glad to have you," said Donald, pouring her some tea.

As they continued to talk, she learned that Donald had been a professor of linguistics and now worked primarily in translation of instructional and warranty information for products with a global distribution.

She turned to Zachary and asked about his current work, since she couldn't imagine why he'd have left Los Angeles if he was so successful in the entertainment business.

"I guess it seems strange to someone in the performing arts business that I would leave LA when I was experiencing success," Zachary said. "I must confess I left for personal reasons rather than anything to do with my profession. The environment became very toxic for me.

"Lots of drugs everywhere and lots of money to buy them. I was finding it difficult to resist the urging of my collaborators and eventually got myself into, um, trouble with cocaine. I went into rehab at the Betty Ford and came out clean, but I knew I needed to get out of the environment I had been in if I was to stay that way. I was looking for alternatives when I came across a blog that Frances had started. It focused on meditation and recovery. I had a side chat with her online after one of her sessions, and she invited me to visit her *compound*, and that's where we're sitting now—Frances's compound," Zach said with a chuckle.

"We have about a half hour before our midday meal, Emma," Donald said. "You are welcome to tour the house now, or we can continue to visit if you'd like. We want you to feel that you've had time to ask any questions you might have to help you form an impression of our little community by the time you leave. It is our understanding you will be taking the three o'clock train back into the city, and we want to make sure you are on the train and settled by two forty-five. We will plan accordingly."

"Well, thank you so much," Emma replied. "I think I'd like to visit a bit longer before lunch and see the house after we eat."

"Certainly. What is it we can tell you?" asked Donald.

"Well, how does this all work? That is, is it a boarding house? Who owns it? Does Frances run it? And how much is the rent? I understand each person has their own room and meals are included. Is that correct?"

Zachary and Donald both smiled and laughed politely.

"All rational questions, Emma. But this isn't a rational place," said Zachary.

●ᵜ∴•

Donald explained to Emma that there was no rent. "Frances owns the house and the property. It has been in her family for a long, long time. If you live here, you live here as her guest—as part of her family, really."

Zachary added, "We who live here have a couple things in common. We need to live in a healthy environment, and we need family to support our personal growth. We have each lost our way at one time or another, including Frances. Her way of finding peace has been to create an environment where the world does not encroach and cannot rob each of us of that which is our gift. We are here to heal and to be nurtured … by each other. That has been a missing piece for all of us."

"As we each begin to reap benefits from our specific talents, we do, of course, contribute to the household," Donald added. "Frances believes that we will each blossom and grow, given the right surroundings. She has no doubt that we will grow together as a family as well as into productive human beings. That is her vision. Zachary and I are the first, but there will be more. This house is large."

Emma was speechless, which was well timed since just at this moment, a dinner bell tinkled from the other room. Zachary said, "Lunch is served. Welcome to the Ritz."

They proceeded into the dining room, where a magnificent quiche—yes, magnificent—was in the center of the beautifully set table. Small dishes of fruit were set at each place, and a lemon tart on an elegant serving dish sat on the sideboard, waiting for its moment in the sun, so to speak.

Frances directed Emma to her place. The others knew which places were theirs. They bowed their heads for a moment, sitting in silence for those who wished to give thanks. Frances served each person a generous piece of the magnificent quiche, and for a bit, the room grew quiet.

"I, uh, want to thank you, Frances, for inviting me into your lovely home," said Emma, when they had set down their forks. "You see, I have been looking for a place to settle. My life has been chaotic for a while now, and I need time to stop and think about where to go from here. That's why I spoke with you online initially.

"I have to say that I'm having a hard time believing what I'm seeing here though," Emma continued. "Is this real or some kind of scam? Because I promise, if it's a scam, I have absolutely nothing for anyone to take advantage of. No money, no family connections, no friends, no property, no education. All I have is the small success I've had on stage, and that wasn't sustainable because my life outside of acting was so unstable. As I've said, I feel like I have to finish growing up before I can be the adult everyone expects me to be, but I have no place to do that. When I connected with you, Frances, I was looking for a cheap apartment, probably in a terrible neighborhood, because that's all I'd be able to afford. I figured I'd live alone, because that's the only way I could be sure my surroundings would be stable.

"I guess what I'm saying is that I would love to join you here if this place is real. In fact, I have a friend named Angela who is in a terrible relationship, even threatening I'd say, who was going to come with me today, but she couldn't get away from her partner to join me. She needs this place too.

"I know that was incredibly inappropriate," said Emma, "but we aren't exactly in the real world here, and Angela is truly in need, so I put it out there."

Frances listened without reacting, again with that look of peace on her face. "Lemon tart, dear?"

To avoid being any more impolite than she had already been, she nodded enthusiastically as Frances arose, gracefully moved to the sideboard, and served pieces of picture-perfect lemon tart on Wedgewood china dessert plates.

Pouring coffee for each person at the table, Frances said, "I would like you to look around the house with Zachary, dear. After that, I will take you to the train. How did you find the quiche?" asked Frances.

"I loved it," said Emma. "I can't think of anything I've eaten, ever, that tasted better to me—except maybe this lemon tart."

"Well, as I said," intoned Zachary, "welcome to the Ritz."

When they'd finished with dessert, Zachary pulled out her chair. Emma stood up, put her napkin on the back of her chair, and they headed toward the foyer. The stairs weren't just normal stairs of course. The newel post looked like something out of Windsor Castle. And the stairs were high gloss, white oak, stained dark. Carpet treads were fixed to each step with a bronze bar to hold them taut. As they ascended, Emma thought she'd only seen this type of décor in the best theatres in New York, where she'd auditioned a few different times.

"There are six bedrooms up here," Zachary said, "which is why I think Frances will ultimately invite six guests to live and work here. At the front of the house is the owner's suite, where Frances sleeps. It was her parents' room at one time, her grandparents' before them, and her great-grandparents' before that. Her family goes back many generations in this house."

"Wow!" Emma exclaimed. "How cool is that? To live in the very same space as your ancestors from a hundred years ago."

"Opposite Frances's suite is Professor Fernandez's. And these two hallways," Zachary said, pointing diagonally to the right and the left, "have two bedrooms each. That makes six rooms, or suites really. I'll show you one of the empty ones."

Moving down the hallway to the right, Zachary opened a door. It led into a bright room with large windows that had swirls in the glass, meaning, explained Zachary, they were very old. Light yellow curtains were on each of two windows, and they looked like satin to Emma. Satin curtains! In between those windows was a window seat with lush cushions covered in a cheerful floral pattern that perfectly complemented the curtains. It was a beautiful retreat for reading, napping, studying scripts, or just being. A covering on the window made it look like it was covered with paper from the outside, but on the inside, there was a perfectly clear view, and sunlight shone in, kind of like those advertisements on city buses that cover the outside windows, but passengers can still see out, and light can get in. The yard, wild and overgrown, abandoned, reinforced that this house was also abandoned. But the sky out there was big and blue, and Emma thought the stars would be beautiful at night.

"Just think," she said to Zachary, "of all the cars that speed by this place daily. They have no idea about this house or the people in it."

Zachary nodded and smiled. "Exactly," he said.

The bedroom had an oval outside wall. The ceiling was probably twelve feet high, with crown molding around. The floor was a dark, rich wood, covered with a beautiful Persian rug. The walls were creamy white. A queen-sized bed sat in the middle of the room, with nightstands on either side, each with a milk glass lamp. An overstuffed chair in the corner, with a large ottoman, was so inviting she felt like plopping down into it. And finally, two doors, one leading to a nice-sized closet, or really a changing room–closet combination, and the other into a bathroom. The bathroom had a beehive pattern black-and-white tile on the floor, a clawfoot tub, and a large, round sink with a wooden medicine cabinet and mirror centered above it. It had huge faucets, the left one with an H on the handle and the right one with a C on it. It was the coolest place Emma had ever seen.

"Yep, so this is pretty much the same as the other three bedrooms," Zachary explained. "They all have their own bathroom, window seat, overstuffed chair, and are the closest thing to a hug I can imagine in the material world."

If he is a bad guy in disguise, Emma thought, *my Spidey sense isn't picking up on it.*

"Lovely," she said. "Absolutely lovely."

Pouring a second cup of coffee for each of them, Frances sat down, looked at Donald, and asked, "Is she one of us, dear?"

She and Donald had a rapport that spanned decades. They communicated almost telepathically. Although just a few years older than Frances, Donald was the most senior member of the household, and she trusted his judgment—and loved him dearly.

"Yes, I think so."

"And what about her friend—Angela, I believe? Shall we invite her friend along next time?" Frances asked.

"Yes, I think so," said Donald again. "We may have to strategize a bit if the young woman is afraid of her partner and unable to get away."

"Yes, I had the same thought," Frances agreed. "We'd need to set up something to pull him away. I can ask Emma about that in the car on the way back to the train. I'll also get an idea about whether she is willing to take a chance on us. She may think we're the real-life Addams family."

"Indeed," said Donald, smiling. "We may be."

Angela McCall was born and raised on the South Side of Chicago. She came from a big Catholic family of eleven children. She was ninth in birth order and always had the feeling her parents were tired of having and raising kids by the time she came along. They worked all day, every day, until they were exhausted; her father outside the house, and her mother inside the house. And that was just to put food on the table and keep a roof over their heads. The older kids raised the younger kids. After the older kids moved out, her mother took a job outside the house, and the younger kids were pretty much on their own. Angela was one of the younger kids.

Angela was a good student. She was tall and athletic. She had strawberry-blond hair, blue eyes, and a pretty smile. She also talked like she'd been raised on the South Side of Chicago. The McCall family was a fixture in their neighborhood. They had all gone to the same Catholic schools, with a McCall in every grade and in every sport.

When the boys graduated, they got union or labor jobs. The girls got office or retail jobs. After a few years as an administrative assistant at a hospital, where everyone came to her for IT help, Angela decided to try to do something more. She signed up for classes at the community college, determined to do something other than wait tables for the rest of her life. She knew she had a gift for technology. She was an IT prodigy at her small high school, which didn't mean much in the real world, but it gave her something to pursue. She did seem to have an innate understanding of computers—what they could do and how to use them to do it. She was on track to graduate from the yearlong program with perfect grades.

To support herself and pay her tuition, she worked in the evenings at the local Subway, which is where she first met Emma. It was also where she first met Rooney.

Rooney Hardy was from the neighborhood but ten years older than Angela—same age as her brother Pat. He came into the store regularly and began chatting her up.

When he asked, "What's a beautiful girl like you doing in a place like this?" she told him it was temporary.

"I'm in school. This job is to pay tuition. When I graduate in the spring, I'm outta here," she told him. A few months later, toward the end of the school year, Rooney came in and offered her a job in IT at his company, with a salary she had only ever dreamed about. Her brothers were making that much in their union jobs. This was too good to be true.

She shared the news with her brothers, specifically her brother Pat, who was in the same graduating class as Rooney. "He wasn't the nicest guy" was Pat's response.

"I'm not marrying him. I'm going to work for his company, Pat. I doubt I'll have anything to do with him. It will look like a great first job on my résumé, and I don't have to stay there forever," she replied.

And that was how she got involved with Rooney, first as an employee and then as a romantic partner. He worked on her and worked on her, until she finally agreed to a date with him. He showered her with gifts, flowers, clothes, jewelry—basically love-bombing her. They went out a few times, and he was a perfect gentleman and treated her like a queen. He took her to expensive restaurants and openings of exhibits, where all the attendees had money, if the jewelry they were wearing was the real thing.

After a few months, he suggested she move into his beautiful house with him.

Angela was still commuting to work from her parents' home, although her parents had retired out west and only stayed in the house when they came to town. Her younger sister, Lucy, also lived in the house. Angela was still sleeping in the bedroom she'd shared with her sisters growing up. This seemed like an opportunity to get out of the house and join the adult world. Rooney was introducing her to a world she had only ever seen on TV. In retrospect, she could see the signs of his controlling behavior, but as a twenty-three-year-old dealing with a thirty-three-year-old narcissist, she did not.

Things changed as soon as she moved in with Rooney. He was surly and critical of everything she did. While continuing to treat her like royalty when they were out socially, she spent most of her time when they were alone trying to anticipate what mood he'd be in so she could do whatever it would take to keep him from going off on her. She was stressed out and, if she was honest, scared all the time.

The other problem was that she sensed Rooney's business dealings were not completely legitimate. She couldn't figure out from the financials, which she saw because she entered financial data into the software she'd customized for him and ran reports for him. She couldn't tell exactly what was going on, but whatever it was, it involved a lot of transporting of goods across borders and cash transactions. It just didn't sit right with her. And when she asked him about it, even indirectly, he'd become verbally abusive. One day, when they were alone in the office, she asked him about a transaction, and he threw something at her, reminding her that she worked for him and not the other way around.

She wanted to get out of this job and this relationship, but he controlled her time and her money. It had only been six months, and she felt as though she'd been in this situation for six years.

And he insisted on accompanying her to any social gatherings with friends or family. He was more predictable among people he was trying to impress but could be volatile with people he felt could see through him or who had no value to him. The latter included her friends and family, so she often begged off, telling them she had a conflict. She doubted her sisters and her friends wanted Rooney with them for girls' night out. As a result, she felt even more isolated and vulnerable.

She knew she had to do something after a recent incident at work. One evening, after everyone had left, he began nuzzling her neck and telling her how beautiful she was and how much he loved her, saying, "You know we belong together, and if you ever tried to leave me, I'd do whatever I needed to do to keep you." It wasn't said in a romantic way but rather in a threatening way. She knew she had to figure out a way to get out of there.

One day, Angela ran out to pick up lunch for the office staff. She passed the Subway where she'd worked and decided to stop to get sandwiches and see who was still there from the old crew. Emma was working, and since it was midafternoon, the store wasn't busy. She and Emma had always enjoyed working the same shift together. They had always had an easy rapport and seemed to understand each other. Emma was excited to see her but commented on how thin Angela had become. "Everything OK?" she asked.

At that point, Angela began talking and couldn't seem to stop until she had told Emma everything.

"He's controlling. I'm afraid to stay with him but afraid of what he'd do if I tried to leave. My gut is also telling me he's involved in something illegal, and I don't want to be around it or have any part of it. If that's not all bad enough, I'm also concerned that from his point of view, I know enough about what goes on at the business that I'd be a threat to him if I tried to leave."

Emma excused herself to take care of a customer.

When she returned, she said, "I know of a place. I am visiting there myself this weekend. I was looking around on the internet for someplace to go to get out of the city, where I could gather my thoughts about my next move. I Googled, 'Rooms for Rent, South Suburbs,' and ended up in a chat room where a woman named Frances asked me to go to a side chat to discuss my situation. I told her a bit about my background, and she invited me to visit. I think you should come with me."

Angela didn't know exactly what Emma's background was, but she knew she'd been an actress—a starving one, as they say. She believed this opportunity was an answer to her prayers and wanted to see the place, but she wasn't sure how to get away over the weekend without Rooney.

"I'd love to go with you, but I'll have to wait to see how the weekend goes. If Rooney's home, I can't go anywhere without him. He insists on driving me and waits for me. I am a prisoner for all intents and purposes. So just let me see if by some chance he has a business meeting or something else that would take him out for a while. I'll call you if I can get away. If I can't, I'll stop by next week to find out what you thought of the place."

And that's the way they left it.

•⁖·•

Emma didn't hear from Angela and visited the house alone. Each day the week after her visit to the house, Emma hoped that Angela would be able to stop by Subway, and it happened the following Thursday. She came in to pick up lunch for the office staff again. It was clear to Emma that Angela was on a short leash for errands like this, with Rooney keeping tabs on how long she was out without his direct supervision.

Emma was busy with customers when Angela came in, since it was closer to the lunch hour than the last time she'd come by. As Angela's turn in line brought her close enough to Emma to talk, she handed Emma a note with the orders for her coworkers. Emma talked softly as she prepared sandwiches.

"I have found the perfect place for myself, and I think for you as well," Emma said excitedly but under her breath.

"At this point, I just need to get away," Angela answered. "And going home or anywhere in the neighborhood, even though my brothers are around, would not be safe. I need someplace where Rooney wouldn't think to look."

"Well, this place is far enough out of the city and really kind of off the grid, so I think it fits that description," Emma replied. "I mentioned that I had a friend, and the owner said they'd like to meet you and would, uh, be willing to help you visit."

"How could they do that?" Angela asked.

"I don't know," said Emma. "But after meeting them, I believe they can do just about anything. And I would love for you to see this place. They have invited me, or rather, Frances, the lady who owns it, has invited me to move in. It all feels too good to be true. I'd feel better if you saw it too and could give me your reaction. I'm trying not to get myself involved in any more chaos. I've had enough chaos."

"I'm with you there," Angela said. "I would love to see this place and share my impressions with you. But I don't know how I can get free for a few hours to go with you."

"Let me email Frances to let her know you're interested. I'll find out what she has in mind. Call in with your order next week, and I'll let you know what she says. You won't have to say anything; I'll just let you know what she says. I'm here every day next week. In the meantime, be aware of an opportunity to break away. There's hope, Angela. I can feel it." With that, Emma handed a big bag of sandwiches to the cashier. Angela paid and headed out of the store.

Angela was able to call Emma midweek with an order for the office staff. Someone whose voice she didn't recognize answered. She asked for Emma by name. She had to wait a bit until Emma finished getting food pans filled for the noon rush.

"This is Emma," she said. "How may I help you?"

"Hi. My name is Angela, and I have an order for six sandwiches. One of my coworkers will pick up the order at eleven thirty."

"Got it," Emma said. "I'm so glad you called. I have great news. You give me a sandwich order and then wait a bit, like I'm writing it down. I'll fill you in on my conversation with Frances in between sandwiches. So go ahead with the first order."

"Okay. The first is a footlong with tuna. She'd like tomato, onion, and white cheese on it. A bag of regular chips too please," Angela said.

Emma quickly said, "Rooney goes out for a massage every Saturday, right? And every other Saturday, he gets a haircut as well, so he's out most of the morning? And this Saturday is one of those mornings?"

"Yes, that's correct," Angela answered, wondering how she knew that.

"Frances said to leave when he leaves. We'll take the train together from the subway station by the Art Institute, to University Park. I'll meet you in the station. You will be home by noon, before Rooney gets back. Item number two?"

"Oh, yes. I'd like a salad with turkey and all the vegetables except banana peppers. And ranch dressing."

"Don't ask me how they do it or how they know Rooney's schedule. I know this sounds creepy, and that makes these people seem even creepier, but just meet them and make up your own mind. Item number three?"

"A *wrap*," Angela said, with much greater force than she had intended. "Uh, a veggie wrap, with honey mustard. And a chocolate chip cookie. And regular chips."

"I know you're skeptical and frightened. Don't be. You'll be safe, and we'll be together. I'll meet you at the station, and we'll catch the 8:00 a.m. train. Next?"

When the sixth item had been ordered, Emma attempted to reassure Angela again. Angela was clearly terrified. She was being asked to trust unknown people, who had a plan she knew nothing about, based on information they'd gotten—how? And from whom? She was afraid of Rooney and knew his constant suspicions gave him an almost sixth sense bordering on paranoia. She'd have to decide whether she was desperate enough to trust Emma's judgment. And face it, she didn't really know Emma that well. She liked her, but how did she know her judgment was good about these people? She had only just met them.

"At least I'll have a few days to think about it," Angela reassured herself.

On Friday night, Angela and Rooney were walking into Gene and Georgetti Steak House downtown when Rooney excused himself to go into the restroom. Angela had noticed a man sitting in the lobby who'd made eye contact with Rooney when they first walked in and then headed in the direction of the restroom. She wondered if Rooney knew that man.

She sat in a chair, watching the people move through the restaurant, wishing the walls could talk. Gene and Georgetti had been in business in the city for eighty years. She imagined a lot of Chicago history had been made over dinner in this place.

About five minutes passed, and Rooney came back, seeming agitated. It was times like these she was literally afraid of him.

"We're leaving," he said sharply. She knew better than to ask any questions. She followed him out the door, waiting while the valet got Rooney's keys. They hadn't even gotten the car parked yet, so Rooney simply walked over to it and began to get in, without tipping the valet. Angela slipped the valet five dollars and thanked him.

Rooney yelled to her impatiently, "Let's go!"

She hurried to the car, jumped in, and he sped off.

"Is everything OK?" she asked.

"I don't need to explain anything to you, remember?" he hissed.

"Of course, you don't. I was just asking out of concern," she said.

"Enough!" he shouted. "I am not in the mood for a chat, if you're too stupid to notice."

At that point, she determined that she'd do whatever it took to meet Emma at that train tomorrow. She needed to get away from this unstable asshole.

When they got back to Rooney's, she quietly retreated to the den while he went into his office. She planned to fall asleep on the sofa while watching the midnight movie. Tomorrow morning couldn't come soon enough.

The next day, when Angela woke in the den, the TV was still on, volume low. It seemed strange to her that Rooney hadn't stopped in to give her tasks to attend to during the morning while he'd be gone. It was his way of controlling her time even when she wasn't with him, she knew.

Maybe it was a good thing he'd been mad at her last night. Maybe he didn't want to talk to her.

She got up and walked into the hallway of the large home Rooney had lived in by himself when she met him. He had apparently had a partner prior to her, but that person was someone they did not speak about. In fact, she wouldn't have known about the prior relationship at all had one of Rooney's colleagues not called her by that name when they ran into him at a restaurant. The name was Charlotte. She'd never forget that.

Rooney's housekeeper, Olivia, was in the next room. She came several times each week to clean, make a grocery run, and to do anything else Rooney assigned to her on a running list of chores. Angela greeted her and asked if she'd seen Mr. Rooney before he'd left for his Saturday-morning routine.

"Yes, ma'am," Olivia responded. "I packed his things. He was leaving for Texas. He said he'd be back tonight or tomorrow."

"Oh," Angela said quietly. "Thank you, Olivia," she said as she checked her phone, thinking he'd have left her a text with errands for the morning.

"I'll be out this morning doing my regular errands. Did he leave a list for me by chance?" she asked.

"No, ma'am," Olivia responded. "No list today."

"OK. Thank you. And thank you for keeping this household running. You do a great job, and I appreciate it very much," Angela said. She thought someone should talk to the woman like a human being instead of a slave. Rooney certainly wasn't going to do it.

As she made her way upstairs to the main suite, she

mused over how early Rooney had left and that he had not given her instructions for his time away from her—very unusual behavior for him.

These people are very good, she thought, thinking of Emma's friends as she quickly showered and left the house. The Uber she had ordered was waiting for her in front of the house. She jumped into the car and was at the station on time, where she found Emma waiting. It was 7:50 a.m.

"I'll need to grab a coffee on the train," she said, looking longingly at Emma's cup.

"Nope. I have one for you here. I didn't know if you wanted anything in it, so here are some packets of cream and sugar. Let's get on the train."

* * *

Angela and Emma settled into their seats on the train in a car that was almost empty. The city was not up and hopping on the train at eight o'clock on a Saturday morning.

"How did it go this morning?" Emma asked Angela. "Was Rooney occupied? Is that how you got out of the house?"

"Oddly enough," Angela said, still a bit unnerved, "he left suddenly for Texas this morning. I only knew about it from the housekeeper. He was in quite the nasty mood last night, so I 'accidentally' fell asleep in front of the TV and spent the night in the den. He was gone when I got up."

"Really? Wow. I wonder how they made that happen," Emma responded. "We'll find out when we get there. But how are you doing?"

"I'm terrified," Angela said. "Really scared. If I didn't

have to go back, I wouldn't. He's made some scary remarks recently, almost as though he can tell what I'm thinking … and I'm thinking I want to get away from him."

"Maybe you shouldn't go back then," Emma said. "Why do you have to go back?"

"Well, first of all, where can I go that he can't find me?" she answered. "And then there are my clothes. And my bank account. I have direct deposit for my paycheck. Can that be traced if he filed a missing person's report on me and I had been taking out money? I'm afraid of him, and I know I have good reason to be. I'm not sure what happened to Charlotte, his girlfriend before me, but I know it is forbidden to mention her name, and there is no trace of her. And she lived in that house with him. Maybe I'm just spooked, but I am truly frightened."

"Well, one thing at a time. Let's deal with what we can today. If you get the same feeling I get from these people, we may be able to discuss this with them," Emma said, trying to sound encouraging, while at the same time worrying if Frances might not want to become involved with someone who was being stalked by a volatile person. The whole idea of Frances's community was to get away from volatility. Emma didn't know where Angela would be able to find safety, and now she was scared too.

When they reached the parking lot, Emma was thrilled to see Frances's large black truck waiting for them. She pointed it out to Angela, and they moved quickly from the train to the truck; now they were both nervous wrecks.

"Hello, ladies!" Frances said cheerfully. "I'm so excited to see you again, Emma, and to meet you, Angela. Thank you for coming to visit us. As Emma may have mentioned, we don't have a lot of company, so it's a big event for us, and I felt inclined to whip up a lovely breakfast in honor of your visit."

Emma had meant to mention the cuisine to Angela, but their conversation made the time on the train fly by, and before they knew it, they were in the parking lot. She just hoped their stomachs would settle down so they could eat.

She had also failed to mention the abandoned house and the lost road and the boarded-up back door and having to hop between rotten boards to get into the house. Good thing Angela was concentrated on getting someplace safe and at this point didn't care if it was an abandoned house in the middle of nowhere.

Then they stepped into the kitchen. Emma heard a gasp from Angela. It reminded her of decompression. It occurred to Emma that Angela might have been holding her breath for a long time.

"Well, my dears," Frances said, "I am once again going to direct you to the living room to meet some of the other residents while I finish preparing our meal. And, Emma, you and Zachary can do the tour for Angela. We'll have brunch at ten o'clock, which will give you almost an hour to chat and walk around. I want to get you back to the train by eleven thirty in order to get Angela back home by one o'clock. Does that sound workable to you both?"

"Yes. Yes, it sounds perfect. Thank you so much," gushed Angela. Her fears lifted as she moved into this house where this lovely woman spoke so kindly. This was the first time she'd felt safe in a long time. She mused over the idea that this unknown place should feel safer to her than the place she spent her everyday life. But it did.

She and Emma moved through the dining room and into the front hallway. They hung up their coats and were greeted by the attractive and sonorous Zachary. "And you must be Angela! We are so pleased to meet you. Thank you for coming!"

"Oh, no," Angela said. "Thank *you* all for having me." They followed Zachary into the living room. Angela's eyes moved around the room in wonder.

As they entered, Donald Fernandez stood up from his wing chair by the fireplace and greeted them as though he'd waited his whole life just to see them. "I am so pleased to meet you, Angela. And to see you again, Emma. Let's get situated so we can answer any questions you may have. May I pour some tea for you?"

"Why, yes, of course, thank you so much," Angela said, with a sense of wonder in her voice. "How kind you all are," she said, almost involuntarily.

"We are grateful," said Donald. "Gratitude will make you kind." And he poured their tea. "I suggest we share a bit about ourselves, and then perhaps you would let us get to know you a bit better, Angela?"

Donald and Zachary gave a bit of background about their lives, and this time, Emma also shared things about her background that Angela did not know.

Then Angela launched into an explanation of her situation, trying to mute some of the more distressing aspects of her current life with Rooney.

"It sounds like a change might benefit you at this point in your life," Zachary uttered.

"Yes," said Donald. "And we could certainly use someone with your expertise here at the house. "Would you consider joining our little family, Angela?"

"I would love to be able to do that," Angela replied. "But my current situation is such that I don't have the freedom to choose what I do. If I were to say I wanted to move, I believe I would be at great risk."

"Then why go back there?" Donald asked.

"Well, actually, Emma and I discussed this on the train," Angela said. "My clothes are there. My bank account is directly linked to Rooney's company, so it would be traceable if I tried to access any of my money, and I would put the people here at risk if Rooney found me here."

"Oh, nonsense," said Donald. "There are plenty of clothes to be bought online. You don't need your clothes, and, in fact, you don't need your money. We have enough money here to sustain you until you are established and begin to make money of your own. Your safety is far more important than any material thing."

Angela's head was reeling. *What?* she thought. These people were not her blood relations. They didn't even know her. Why would they do this?

So she asked, "Why would you all be willing to do this?"

"Well, we're a bit different here," Donald said. "We can't save the whole world, but we can save ourselves and a few more like us. We have all had trouble in our lives, so we know how it happens, and we know what it takes to move beyond it. We also know what a treasure each human being is, and we greatly cherish that."

"We believe in you, Angela," Zachary said. "We only know you from Emma's description and from your situation, but we are willing to take a chance on you if you are willing to take a chance on us."

At that point, the little bell rang in the other room, and the conversation halted. As they all stood to move into the other room, Angela was at a loss for words. She realized that tears were streaming down her cheeks, and she turned to Donald and embraced him. He returned her embrace and said, "Well, let's go see what Frances has for us."

They moved into the dining room to a beautifully set table, with candles and garland down the center. It looked like joy to Angela. On the sideboard, Angela saw what she had been smelling: bacon, sausage, English muffins, waffles, an egg casserole, hash browns, cheese blintzes, and fruit. It was a feast fit for the finest restaurant in Chicago.

Frances directed them to their places at the table to pick up a plate and continue to the buffet, where they struggled to fit everything they wanted to taste onto their plates.

Once they had all returned to their places, and led by Frances, they bowed their heads, each to give thanks in their own way. And then the room grew silent as they enjoyed the feast that had been lovingly prepared for them.

When they finished, Angela found her voice and thanked Frances for the beautiful meal. She asked how they had been able to get Rooney to fly to Texas. Frances and Donald exchanged glances.

"Texas?" Frances said.

"Yes," Angela said. "We were out to eat last night, and Rooney became very upset and insisted we return home immediately. When I tried to ask what was wrong, hoping his anger wasn't going to be directed at me, he told me to mind my own business. In the morning, he left early to catch a flight to Texas. He didn't leave any instructions for me, as he normally would have. He also didn't say when he'd be back."

"Well, we had nothing to do with any of that," Frances said. "I have a friend who is a private detective who observed and reported to us about Rooney's Saturday-morning routine, so we did know he'd be out of the house in the morning. But our plan was to create a delay in that routine having to do with his car," Frances said as she smiled at Donald, "to ensure you'd have plenty of time to get back safely before he returned."

Donald looked at Angela, concerned. "Do you feel safe to return to that home, Angela?"

"No, she doesn't," Emma replied. "I know she doesn't from the conversation we had on the train coming here. Please don't go back there, Angela. You don't have to."

Frances, Donald, Zachary, and Emma all looked at Angela, imploring her to consider herself and her safety.

"I don't know what to do," Angela said. "I'm afraid to go back, and I'm afraid not to go back."

Frances rose from the table and asked Zachary and Emma to take Angela around the house. It was getting close to the time they would need to leave if Angela were to get back on the train and to Rooney's house on time, based on their original plan.

Zachary and Emma stood up. Angela followed them out of the room and to the staircase. At that point, Angela broke down. She sunk onto the second step and sobbed. Zachary sat down on one side of her and Emma on the other. They let her have a good cry.

When she seemed to be ready to move, they rose and walked upstairs. Zachary showed Angela a different room than the one he'd shown Emma, since Emma had brought some of her belongings out with her this time and was moving into that room.

The room he showed Angela was just as lovely and bright. Angela walked around it as though she had landed in wonderland. Could this be a place she could stay? Could she really live here and be safe? Was it fair of her to put these people in jeopardy by dragging them into this mess she had gotten into?

"Isn't this amazing?" Emma asked her. "Wouldn't it be a lovely place to live?"

"Yes," Angela said. "But how can I pay to live here if I can't access my money?"

"Oh," Emma replied as Zachary grinned slightly. "I guess we forgot to go over that. You can pay later."

They walked through to the bathroom and dressing room, then moved toward the door. Without uttering a word, they descended to the dining room, where Frances and Donald sat together, having a cup of tea.

Frances said, "Well, what do you think, Angela? Will you join us?"

"And we think you should just stay rather than trying

to find another time to break away from your current situation," Donald said. "It's too risky."

"Yes," Frances said. "I think my PI friend will need to investigate Rooney's activities. Then we'll know if we're dealing with someone who is a harmless bully or someone who is dangerous. In the meantime, you can stay safely here with us. Please be assured that you may leave at any time. We are not keeping you here; rather, we are offering you refuge for the time being and for as long as you wish to stay."

And that was that.

Rooney returned home late in the afternoon on the Saturday Emma took Angela to the house. He was in a foul mood when he entered the house. He shouted, "Angela, get down here."

But there was no response, and when he searched the house, he found no Angela. Her clothes were there, but her purse was gone. Had she gone out with her idiot sisters? She knew he would not be good with that. She was going to need to have a review of some of the fundamentals when she got in, which he assumed would be soon. Surely, she wouldn't go out against his wishes and then stay out beyond dinnertime. Not unless she was really testing who was boss. And there was no doubt in his mind who was boss. "She'll need a lesson," he said to himself.

He didn't need this crap right now. His business dealings in Texas had hit some snags, and he had gone down to straighten them out, only to find the area crawling with cops and immigration officials. He quickly got out of town. But there went a ton of money he was counting on for investment in another shipment.

It was one thing, he thought, to have to deal with this crap outside his house. He was not going to deal with it inside his house. Where was Angela? He was now looking forward to setting her straight.

In the meantime, Angela and Emma were like two schoolgirls, running back and forth between their rooms as they settled in. At 6:00 p.m., the dinner bell rang, and they headed downstairs, looking forward to the food and the company at the table for the first time in a long time.

Frances and Donald sat at either end of the table. There were two chairs on each side, and Frances directed Angela to the side where Zachary sat, and Emma to the other side.

The food on the sideboard not only smelled like heaven but also looked like heaven. The group bowed their heads and silently did whatever each of them did during that time. Frances asked Donald to lead, and he rose to serve himself. The others followed.

When they had their plates, it was difficult to wait for the last person to be seated to eat, but they did. Then all talking ceased, and the feast was in full bloom—salmon with mustard sauce, garlic mashed potatoes with chives and cheeses, broccoli, and homemade rolls. It was amazing.

After dinner, the group sat for a while, sipping coffee and chatting. Angela had to admit that while she felt like she was in some sort of cocoon, she had a lot of fear deep down inside. She knew Rooney would not be happy when he came home and she wasn't there. And she knew all too well what "Rooney not happy" looked like. She hoped he wouldn't be able to find her here. What choice did she have but to leave? It was done now, and she had no desire to go back. So she would play it out, whatever that meant.

CHAPTER 10

The snow had indeed kept most of the staff at home. Helen was getting so much done. She reported on Marty's status, and all seemed well for now. She needed to work on his absence from his residence and see how to handle the paperwork on that. She knew he was safe, but the system didn't recognize the place he was staying as a legitimate transitional house. She was still concerned about his check-in dates and how he'd handle those, but she'd deal with that when the time came. As it was, his next check-in date was Friday, and depending upon the weather, she'd either see him at the house or via Zoom.

In the meantime, she decided to dig through some databases to see if she could learn more about any of the residents, beginning with Frances. Helen thought about her elegant presence and what an amazing lady she seemed to be.

Helen also needed to catch up with Ryan after 4:00 p.m. when the market closed. He'd be working from home today. The glories of technology. No more snow days for workers or school kids. Poor kids.

That situation needed some work. She shouldn't have felt so relieved to be unable to join Ryan on Friday and to be unable to spend any time with him over the weekend. In college, they'd been inseparable. Now that they were in their own apartments and could be together whenever they weren't working, without supervision, she was preoccupied, and he seemed to interfere with whatever it was she was preoccupied with. He didn't appear to mind the distance either. Yep, the situation needed attention.

She'd talk to him later today. Right now, she had to move forward with all the clients whose paperwork she'd completed over the weekend, beginning with Maggie Dax, a repeat offender the other caseworkers had assigned to Helen, since they'd all had a turn with her already. Maggie should be moving off Helen's caseload this spring, and it wouldn't be a moment too soon.

Maggie was a kid who'd been raised in the foster care system. Sadly, she'd learned coping skills in her chaotic early life that led to trouble no matter where she was placed. She lied. She ran away. She stole things. She drank, smoked cigarettes, did drugs when available, and prostituted herself when she was short of funds. It was a mess, and there didn't seem to be any way to get into her head that there were other options, other choices she could make.

The thing about Maggie that irked all the caseworkers whose charge she had been was that Maggie was a very, very bright young lady. Her IQ tested in the 150s. Maggie could have the cure for cancer lurking somewhere behind her unproductive coping mechanisms, but no one could figure out how to reach that side of her. It was discouraging, and Helen knew she'd been assigned Maggie by Tom to teach her that some of her clients just couldn't come out of the fog they had learned to live in to cope with their lives. And, just maybe, Tom was hoping that she would somehow be able to get through to Maggie. He and the others had been disappointed many times by their clients, but they still hoped; she knew they did. They weren't as jaded as they sometimes acted.

Helen was idealistic enough to still look for new strategies to reach Maggie. She read the research on brain development and therapies for those whose brains were in fight-or-flight mode since birth. She'd do her best with Maggie to keep her from ending up back in detention, but she knew she wasn't doing anything that hadn't been done before by her colleagues. Still, she would try.

CHAPTER 11

Ryan Nelson awoke in his best friend, Pete's, apartment. Pete and Ryan had grown up together and were like brothers. It was totally comfortable for Ryan to be sleeping on the couch in Pete's sweats, using his laundry room to wash his work clothes from last Friday, and getting ready to use his shower.

It was Monday morning, and he was ready for it. First, the snow was the coolest thing he'd seen in a long time. Second, they'd had the best weekend. This post-college world was better than he could ever have imagined. He had to be at work, but otherwise, no homework, no parents, no grades—it was great.

And he and Pete had met a group of guys from the Board of Trade who were just like they were—ambitious; they wanted to experience life, travel, see everything, do everything. And they saw a lot of guys like themselves who had started out small, saved their money, bought a seat, and made a fortune trading. They were on their way to doing the same.

"And if we don't like the stress," they had decided, "we'll make a boatload of money and get out." They'd heard stories of guys who'd done that, invested the money in real estate, or started their own companies, or bought franchises. It did get hella stressful, especially for the older guys in their forties.

But all of that was for some time in the future. Right now, life was good, even great.

There were drugs around, especially cocaine, because the job required peak attention throughout the day and high energy to stay tuned in to opportunities as they arose, but that wasn't a problem for him. He'd only indulged once or twice. Of course, he hadn't shared that with Helen. She'd flip out. She didn't understand that he wasn't going to end up like one of the dregs she was always so worried about. He was just living it up while he could, experiencing it all. She'd be happy when he made his fortune and they could buy a ranch in Wyoming, or a ski lodge in Colorado, or a sailboat to sail around the world.

Well, time to get to it, he thought. Once again, he'd sorted it all out in his head, and he was on the right path, the path he'd chosen. He'd need to talk to Helen after work. He knew she'd spent the weekend holed up with her three roommates, perfectly content.

She's happy doing that, he thought, *but I need people and more stimulation than that.*

CHAPTER 12

On Monday morning, Johnathan Richards had breakfast and checked out of the club. He cabbed it over to the Drake Hotel for his ten o'clock meeting with Joey. Michigan Avenue was clear of snow, with only slightly less traffic than usual. Amazing city.

He ascended the stairs that led to the lobby at the Drake and called Joey's cell. They were in the Michigan Room. He headed to the elevator with his suit bag. He preferred not to check his personal things if he could avoid it. It was prudent, in his view, to leave as little physical evidence of his visit in the memory of hotel employees as possible, for a variety of reasons.

Joey was waiting with coffee. He and Johnathan sat down together to go over their objectives for the day and their agenda.

"We'll be meeting with Horace Spence at ten o'clock. Horace's operation covers the South Side of Chicago from the lake to Harlem Avenue to the west, and from Twenty-Second Street to the Indiana border to the south. They have a strong outreach and good connections. He's reliable and a great partner.

"At noon, we'll be meeting with James Washington. His people are on the West Side. They cover the lake to Austin Boulevard, bordering Oak Park, Twenty-Second Street to the south, and North Avenue to the north. Again, strong network, effective distribution.

"At four o'clock, we meet with Brian Park. He handles everything north of North Avenue to the Wisconsin border. He will orchestrate the disruption that will distract law enforcement and first responders, allowing us to deliver our shipments to the three distribution points without too much interference."

Johnathan appreciated how clean the plan seemed. He would assess these three individuals when he met them personally. At this point, they had only been told there would be an opportunity they might be interested in. They were coming, the day after a huge snowstorm, negotiating some significant complexity due to the storm and its effect on transportation, to explore that opportunity. That alone spoke well of their command of resources and commitment.

He knew from prior business in Chicago that these individuals ran operations that could turn on a dime. They were dictatorships, not democracies. They didn't have to comply with HR people, labor laws, or annual reviews like other organizations. The command chain was strictly hierarchical, and there were consequences, both good for compliance, in terms of compensation, and bad in the case of ineptitude.

Excusing himself, Johnathan took the last few minutes prior to their first meeting to check his messages and freshen up. He was excited to get these last details set in place and to head back to a more civilized climate and, from his perspective, culture.

Promptly at 10:00 a.m., a stocky, middle-aged man entered the room, addressing Johnathan. "Hey, I'm Horace Spence. Hey, Joey, I didn't see you. How ya doin'?"

Johnathan quickly sized him up. Spence had such a thick Chicago accent that Johnathan had to listen closely to understand him. A native. Well connected. While he had the countenance of a day laborer, Mr. Spence was wearing clothes that shouted money. His hair was perfectly coiffed, his nails manicured, his shoes shined, solid gold Rolex on his left wrist, and a big, shiny diamond ring on his right hand. It was important to this man to be perceived as successful and above the average person by a long shot.

"Great, Horace. Good to see ya, man," Joey responded. "This is our client, Johnny."

"Johnny, how ya doin'?" Horace greeted him.

Now Johnathan wasn't used to being called Johnny, but it was a Chicago thing. Everybody's name was made familiar. It made Johnathan wonder if Horace's family called him Horcy.

"Hello, Mr. Spence," Johnathan said. "I am well, thank you."

Horace looked back at Joey. Now it was Horace who wasn't sure what language was being spoken. Joey pulled it together by steering the conversation to the project at hand.

"Horace, how about giving Johnny here a little background on your operation?"

Spence talked about his labor force, his track record with

former jobs, and the deep market penetration his operatives had on the South Side.

At that point, Joey looked at Johnathan, who nodded. He knew that meant he could share a bit more about the operation they were initiating.

"All three city zones will be involved, north, south, and west, in the distribution of the products," Joey said, addressing Horace. "That product will be five models of guns, the most popular in circulation in the civilian population, including Thompson/Center Arms Encore muzzle-loading rifle, Remington Model 870 pump-action shotgun, Bushmaster AR-15 semiautomatic rifle, Smith & Wesson Model 10 revolver. Since most of the products are large, the boxes they come in will be large. The idea will be to break them down and deliver them to your distributors who can service the clients from satellite locations. We would like your salespeople to get the word out that the materials will be available on February 15, the day after Valentine's Day. We will offload the products from freight trains downtown and into trucks while the police and first responders are busy with a large distraction on Valentine's Day, the fourteenth.

"You can mark up the products as much as your market can bear, Horace, but payment will be due to us at the time of delivery by the trucks to your distribution sites. You'll receive fifteen hundred items, ranging from $1,000 to $30,000 in cost. The bill of lading will itemize what is received, how many of each style, and the respective costs. Payment is to be electronically transferred to an account number that the receiver will get from the delivery person. That will be $10 million due from your site upon delivery.

"Are you interested, Horace?" Joey said in conclusion.

"Absolutely. We are," said Horace. "We won't have a problem selling that amount of firepower. In fact, we could use more. We're in."

They all stood up. It was obvious the meeting was over and that everything that needed to be said at this meeting had been said.

"Wonderful, Mr. Spence," said Johnathan. "I'll leave the scheduling and logistics to you and Joey to finalize. It is a pleasure doing business with you."

"Yeah, we'll talk soon, Hor. Be careful on the streets; they could be getting icy," added Joey.

It was 10:30 a.m., and a third of the project was in place without a problem. If all three meetings went like this, Johnathan would be sipping a martini in the executive club at O'Hare by 5:00 p.m.

At five minutes to noon, a small black man with the look of an accountant entered the Michigan Room at the Drake. Johnathan and Joey both stood and greeted James Washington.

Joey began the meeting by saying that James had been born and raised on the West Side of Chicago and ran his business like a Fortune 500 company.

"I take structure very seriously," explained Mr. Washington. "I am an accountant by training. And since I am primarily a numbers guy, the sooner we get to the finances, the better," he concluded.

Johnathan liked this guy immediately. He was all

business with very little chatter. If all his meetings were this on point, there'd be a lot more time for leisure in this life.

Joey explained the plan, as he had done with Horace.

Washington took out his calculator and said to himself, "Fifteen hundred items, $10,000,000 due at delivery. Got it. Sounds good. We should be able to get a good retail price for those products."

Joey wrapped things up by telling Mr. Washington he'd be in touch with details about the delivery. Mr. Washington nodded to Johnathan and was gone.

"Now that's my kind of meeting," said Johnathan. "Let's order lunch."

⁕ ⁕ ⁕

Brian Park, a dark-complected Asian man with a medium build and somewhat jovial in countenance, walked into the Michigan Room at the Drake Hotel at exactly 4:00 p.m. Johnathan thought it would have made more sense to schedule this meeting earlier in the day, since there was more to talk about than the other two meetings, but if it was as efficient as the others, it wouldn't make a difference.

Brian's people operated their business on the North Side of Chicago from North Avenue to the Wisconsin border. Joey reviewed the plan with Brian, which Brian acknowledged without question. He seemed anxious to get to the larger issue of creating a disruption in the city that would serve as a magnet for police and other first responders.

"You know we need an event to attract the attention of the city in general, Brian. What do you have for us?" Joey asked.

"I've talked with my people, and we have what we believe to be a workable plan to offer," responded Brian. "Since the materials will arrive in the city on February 14, and there are always a lot of people out to dinner on that evening, we think it will be easy to create a disruption. In the tradition of the famous St. Valentine's Day Massacre, we thought we'd stage a mass shooting in a highly populated area. The media will love the date and the story. The public and the pols will be outraged as usual—and totally distracted.

"We can count on numerous casualties requiring emergency services on site, including ambulances, EMTs, and police. The hospitals will be on emergency alert, calling in docs and nurses from surrounding hospitals for the overflow. Police will be everywhere in the area, again, calling in extra cops from other areas of the city to cordon off the perimeter, evacuate people, and look for the shooters.

"My people are professional, so we aren't worried about the reaction or that it will result in any problems for us. And we can use the same kind of weapons we'll be selling, as a sort of product demonstration.

"Do you see any problems with this, or are there any further details you'd like to discuss about the implementation?" Brian asked in conclusion.

"No, no, Brian, thank you," Joey said a bit anxiously. He knew Johnathan didn't like to know much about the activities on the street side of things for these deals. He wanted to know they were in good hands and that the money would be where it was supposed to be. He didn't want to hear all the gory details.

"And then just to confirm, we're talking about an extra

five mil to distribute to my guys when they've completed the job?" asked Brian.

"Right," said Joey, relieved that this meeting seemed to be going quickly and as efficiently as the previous two meetings.

"You and I will talk more about all the details, Bri. I'll be in touch soon. And thanks for coming. You are a great partner, and I know you and your organization will do everything exactly the way you've described. That St. Valentine's Massacre *coincidence* is a great detail. You guys are getting creative—or nostalgic. One or the other."

With that, Johnathan stood, signaling that the meeting was over. The three men shook hands, said their thank yous, and Brian headed out the door.

Joey was a bit apprehensive about Johnathan's reaction to the graphic description of Brian's plan for the fourteenth, but Johnathan just put on his coat, thanked Joey for his great work, and proceeded downstairs for a taxi, thinking about the bar in the concourse at O'Hare and the relaxing business class seat that awaited him for his return trip to LAX.

Johnathan's lack of reaction to the plan made Joey think, *He looks fancy on the outside, but on the inside, he's just like us.*

CHAPTER 13

At 4:15, Ryan called Helen's cell phone. It went to voice mail. "Hi, Lennie. It's me. Call me when you can. Love you."

Helen saw the call when it came through and listened to Ryan's message when she finished the call she had been on. She hit the little phone icon on the message screen, and Ryan answered.

"I missed you this weekend, Len. We all did. Did you get a lot done?" he asked.

"I missed all of you too," she said, wondering if that was true. "I did get a lot done. It was so beautiful outside and so cozy inside. What a great weekend to catch up on work and sleep and hang out with the roommates. How about you?"

"Oh, we spent the weekend in deep intellectual pursuits," Ryan replied sarcastically. "It was a good thing the bar was stocked. I think we played Minecraft for twenty-four hours straight. It was great. But back to it today. I'm still at Pete's. I'll be heading home by five o'clock. Do you want to meet me somewhere for a bite to eat?"

"I'm actually downtown at work," Helen said. "How about we plan to meet when we're both down here. It's easier to meet than it is when you're all the way north and I'm down here. I'm just not real sure how the Els are running. It's either going to be great, because no one came down for work, or they'll be running late because of snow. Does that sound OK?"

"Sure," said Ryan, a bit disappointed. "Tomorrow then. Let's plan on dinner tomorrow."

"Sounds good," Helen replied. "And, Ryan, let's keep it just the two of us. I feel like we need some alone time."

"OK, Len. We can meet after work and grab a cab to Atwood at five thirty then. Love you."

"Love you too," she answered. "Bye."

Helen began to pack up for the day. She put her laptop in her backpack, then put on her heavy coat, hat, gloves, scarf, and boots, which she'd kicked off at about noon. She felt like a Storm Trooper, all geared up to fight the Rebel Alliance. Or maybe like the actor who wore the Wookie suit. *Maybe I shouldn't have watched all the* Star Wars *movies over the weekend*, she thought in passing.

As she walked through the bull pen, she waved to Kevin, who was lovingly interacting with his computer over bits of data. As complex as she found technology, it still had to be easier to be in a relationship with a machine than a person, she thought.

"Night, Tom," she said as she passed Tom's office. He waved her in as he appeared to be wrapping up a phone call.

"Thanks, Rachel. Keep me in the loop please," he said as he hung up.

"I have a bit more intel about what's happening on the street. Do you have a minute?" he asked.

"Yes. Of course," she said as she tried to bend in half to sit in the chair in his office.

"This won't take long," he said. "I can see you'll begin to melt in a matter of minutes, and I don't want a puddle under that chair," he joked.

"It appears that something big is coming to the city. No one is sure when, or what it is, but the scuttlebutt is it will happen during the winter months. Gangs are getting excited. The undercover cops will be interacting with us to keep us informed but also to see whether our population provides any insight into what's up. That's all. You better go. You're getting all red in the face, Helen."

"Thanks Tom. Scary stuff. I'll be sure to bring it up to my clients who are on the street a lot or have gang backgrounds. Careful walking home," she said as she rose from the chair and lumbered toward the elevator.

CHAPTER 14

After work on Tuesday, Ryan walked from the Board of Trade building on Jackson, and Helen came from the Kluczynski building on Dearborn. They grabbed a cab together to Atwood. They'd need to go back for Edith after dinner.

They had discovered this place when they first moved into the city but really couldn't afford it other than on special occasions. It was only recently that Ryan had been making more money and they could eat there once a month or have a cocktail with friends after work.

Ryan was looking forward to seeing Helen and hoped she wouldn't mind that he'd told several of their friends who worked in the area that they'd be there for cocktails. Afterward, they could have dinner alone, as Helen had asked.

When Helen arrived, Ryan was at the bar with several of their friends. They greeted her enthusiastically, and she reciprocated, feeling all the while like her request that they have some alone time had been ignored.

Ryan put his arm around her and kissed her cheek.

"I hope you're OK with a few of the gang meeting us for drinks. We'll have dinner by ourselves, but they were going to be here anyway, so it would be rude to ignore them, especially when they haven't seen you in a few weeks. It's OK, right?"

Helen smiled and turned her attention to one of the women in the group who had asked how she'd gotten home in the storm on Friday. She turned, and they began a conversation.

At about eight o'clock, Helen suggested to Ryan that it was time for her to head home. Since she was driving, the plan had been for her to drop off Ryan after dinner, but they hadn't gotten around to dinner after everyone, except Helen, had a few drinks and the conversation started flowing.

"I'd like to drop you at home if you're ready to leave," Helen said to Ryan.

Ryan, looking, she thought, like a kid who had to leave Six Flags before he was ready, replied, "Uh, sure. I'm ready, Lennie. Let me just say goodbye quickly."

A half hour later, Helen and Ryan headed back to the lot where she'd parked Edith. The downtown streets were quiet now that the working people had headed home. The stoplights seemed extra bright against the piles of snow that lined the streets.

"I'm sorry we didn't get to eat, Len," Ryan said. "Time just got away from us. But wasn't it great to see everyone and just hang out? It's been a while since we've been able to do that together, hasn't it?"

Helen said, "Yes, it has. There's been so much going on at work, and then the weather.

"Ryan," she continued, "I think we need a break. Our lives have changed so much since we were first together; it feels like our attention is being pulled away from the things we shared in common. You're an extrovert, and I'm an introvert, and we used to complement each other, but now that seems to be a liability. When I finish a day filled with people and their problems, I want to go home and be quiet or have a private dinner to unwind. You unwind by being with people. It's just hard right now."

"What?" he said, seeming confused. "I don't understand what taking a break looks like, Len. We are a couple. We have a vision for the future—a plan. And I am working toward that plan, which is why I do what I do. Don't you appreciate that I'm doing everything so you and I can live the dream we've always shared?"

"I'm sorry, Ryan, if this is taking you by surprise. I don't mean to hurt you, but I need a break to figure out who I am in this new space, and I hope you care enough about me to give me a break."

As they pulled up to Ryan's studio apartment in The Logan Square, Helen kissed him on the cheek and told him she'd call to check on him in a few days. Still dazed, Ryan got out of the car, fumbled for his key, and disappeared into his building.

•꙲ꞏ •

Helen had reached out to Ryan the following weekend after she had suggested they take a break. She had texted him to ask if he was doing OK or wanted to talk. It was a long time before he responded, and he said he was out with friends and would catch up with her the next day.

On Sunday, she anticipated a call, but it never came.

On Monday, she checked back after the markets closed, hoping to catch up with him. She left a message, telling him she would understand if he didn't want to talk but that she did want to know that he was OK.

He texted saying, "I'm OK. Thanks for checking."

She guessed that was all she could do at this point. She understood that he had his pride, and she didn't want to impose on that. She had just been sincerely concerned.

She had done some research into past clients and found a full file on Frances. She had indeed lived a fairly detached existence for several years, before disappearing from the roles. Helen had a hard time imagining her on the streets, homeless and vulnerable, while at the same time appreciating the strength of the woman. She had navigated some very rough waters in her life and apparently come out stronger for having done so.

The files also noted that Frances not only inherited some dilapidated old property in the middle of nowhere; she was an heiress. Her net worth had grown and grown over the years, and it became apparent how that house could have been renovated on the inside while looking like a shack on the outside. Helen guessed that the exterior structure was rock solid, while looking like it was about to collapse. Its appearance gave the impression to observers of being worthless and weak, while in fact it was invaluable and strong.

While everyone knows you can't tell a book by its cover,

everyone still does, thought Helen. And that insight into human nature was keeping everyone at the house safe.

At lunch, the staff gathered in the conference room to eat. Some ordered food, and others brought lunch. Kevin was eating kale with sardines. It wreaked. Tom had ordered pizza for himself, Helen, and several others. They sat at the other end of the table from Kevin. The conversation turned to the latest news on the street.

"Have you heard any more about the gang activity, Tom?" Lucia asked. Lucia was a veteran caseworker of Hispanic ethnicity. She had grown up in a neighborhood where gangs were active and often had good insight when rumors started about their activity.

"Well, sort of," Tom replied. "They've heard there will be contraband moved into the city but aren't sure yet if it's guns, drugs, or human beings. We also don't know which areas will be involved—north, south, or central.

"You all could be of great assistance if you'd keep your ears to the ground. Anything you can glean from your clients might help to expose the timing and the plan," he said.

That afternoon, Helen was making client calls when Maggie Dax's name came up. *Oh, I dread this*, she thought. It was almost impossible to reach Maggie most weeks. Eventually, she'd find her, have a very disjointed conversation, and count that as her weekly check-in. But she never felt that she'd reached her on a deeper level.

To her great surprise, Maggie answered the cell phone number she'd given Helen.

"Hi, Helen! What's up?" Maggie asked with more enthusiasm than Helen had ever heard in her voice.

"Just checking up on you, Maggie," Helen replied. "Everything OK?"

"Oh, yeah, great as usual," Maggie replied sarcastically. "I only have a few more weeks of this, right?"

"That's right," Helen replied. "Are you happy about that? You sound happy about something. In fact, I don't think I've ever heard you be happy about anything. What's up?"

"Well, I just bummed a cigarette from a man in a very nice suit, and he offered me twenty dollars and a half an hour off the street, which sounds good to me," she replied.

"Maggie!" Helen urged. "Don't trust people that way. You're going to end up getting hurt."

"JK, Helen. Geez, you're gullible," Maggie chided.

"Ugh," Helen said out loud. "Seriously, Maggie, when are you going to consider, um, a safer lifestyle?"

"Right. I have a lot of choices, Helen. That's why I live like I do," Maggie teased. She'd had many caseworkers over the years, but Helen was her favorite—so innocent, so trusting. She truly believed Maggie had choices. It was endearing, even to Maggie's hardened soul.

"Well, you could help me with something to begin your journey to the straight and narrow," Helen said. "We're hearing rumors of some gang activity coming up. We don't exactly know when, but we're thinking this winter. It would be very helpful if you could keep your ear to the ground and let me know if you hear anything on the street."

"Ahem, that might involve some fraternization that you have previously discouraged me from engaging in,

Helen," Maggie taunted. "Do I have dispensation if I get the information but am arrested while doing it?"

"No, Maggie, no," Helen said, without the patience she had at the beginning of the call. "I don't want you to put yourself at risk. I just want you to keep your ears open and let me know if you hear anything that might save some lives, OK?"

"Sure, like Wonder Woman. I get it, saving a few lives," Maggie replied. "Always glad to help.

"Hang in there, Helen, and don't take off those rose-colored glasses. They are so becoming on you." And Maggie was gone. Helen was always grateful for the end of those calls, at the same time hoping Maggie would still be alive for next week's call. What a way to live.

The day flew by as Helen continued to make calls and catch up with clients. She mentioned the gang business to all of them but knew in her heart that her best bet would be Maggie. No one lived closer to the street than Maggie.

CHAPTER 15

Joey Caruso met with Horace, James, and Brian the week following Johnathan's visit. They understood that a shipment would come into the rail depot on DuSable, in the heart of downtown. This would occur while a disturbance was being created on the North Side in a densely populated restaurant area on Valentine's Day.

The freight would be unloaded onto three trucks and sent to the North, South, and West Sides of the city with bills of lading. They would be unloaded at a designated site, signed for, money transferred electronically, and that would be the end of Johnathan's operation. From that point forward, it would be up to the individual organizers to distribute the products to buyers, some from the city, others from around the country, and still others from outside the country.

The operation had been kept very quiet, given the number of people involved. Professionals in this business understood that their discretion was tied to their livelihood and their lives. Joey was pleased with the plan and confident it would be implemented without a hitch.

CHAPTER 16

It had been several months since Angela and Emma had joined the household, and several weeks since Marty's arrival. The young people, as Donald and Frances called them, seemed to be perfect matches professionally, and they were all doing quite well.

One unique aspect of the house was the unlisted landline. It had been hardwired when Frances did the renovation and listed on the website she maintained. Business contacts requiring conference calls were taken on that line, from the office in the house. It was a safer way to have access to the residents who needed anonymity than a cell phone in their name. When they needed a cell phone, they used a burner. It all worked, although a landline was an artifact from a bygone era to the younger members of the household.

The phone seldom rang, but one day when Zachary was leaving the kitchen with a snack, he passed the office just as the phone began to ring. He ducked into the office and engaged with the unfamiliar device.

"Hello," he said, somewhat hesitantly. These phones attached to walls were weird things.

"Hello," a voice said, with an Irish accent. "I'd like to talk with Marty or Zachary about a song."

"Of course. This is Zachary. Which tune are you interested in? And just a minute if you don't mind. I'd like to get Marty in here, just in case you have any questions about the music. We cowrite the tunes. He does the music, and I do the lyrics. Who may I say is calling?" Zachary asked.

"It's Paul Hewson."

Zachary put down the phone and ran to the living room where Marty was playing a catchy new tune on the piano. Zachary was out of breath and at risk of choking on the banana he had been eating. "Marty! Come quick! Bono's on the phone! He's interested in one of our songs!"

Marty looked at Zachary incredulously. "Right. Bono. I'll be right there. I gotta write this down."

"No, dude. I'm serious. Now."

Marty jumped up and ran after Zachary, afraid he was having some sort of acid flashback. When they reached the office, Zachary put the call on conference and asked if the gentleman was still on the line.

"Yes, I am. I would like to purchase the rights to record the tune 'Preacher.' I heard it on your site. You guys have some great stuff. It's original and fresh. We may record it with a quicker tempo than you did and more electric sound, but it will still have a hint of the ballad in it," Bono said. "And what would be the cost?"

"Uh, $30,000," Zachary said, "and 2 percent of future royalties." He'd just made that up. Marty sat down with a thud on the lovely chintz covered chair.

"Great," Bono replied. "Have your legal stuff sent to our

agent's office in London—it's Winchester Associates—and we'll transfer the signed docs and fees. Great to talk with you both. And best wishes."

Zachary had been rather skeptical about landlines prior to this call, but he was now a full-on fan. The duo couldn't wait to share the news at dinner tonight. The joy of sharing good news was one of the happiest by-products of living at the house.

CHAPTER 17

Maggie Dax walked down Western Avenue, wearing an old coat she'd gotten the last time she'd dined at the Salvation Army. She had a bad experience under the bridge at Fullerton and the Kennedy Expressway. She needed to get away from there for a few days. It was freezing cold in Chicago in the winter, and it was everyone for themselves. She knew she could talk to Helen about staying in a transitional community, but she'd kind of burned her bridges in most of them over the years. They weren't receptive to taking her in, and she wasn't receptive to being taken in by them. This life was getting worse each day though, in correlation with her age. It had been easier when she was younger and had more resilience. She felt like she was twenty-two going on sixty.

She had twenty dollars from sitting by the exit ramp from the highway yesterday and decided to step into a diner called Morning Mouth Café on Addison and Western for some warm breakfast food and a respite from the cold.

The proprietors weren't too excited about her arrival, but she showed them her cash, and they couldn't turn her away. They seated her at the back of the restaurant. She knew she smelled like stale smoke and body odor. She'd need to head to the women's shelter next to get something clean to wear and to take a shower. The problem with that was the line. She might wait two days in line outside in the cold for her turn to use the shower and still have to find somewhere to sleep, but she didn't have an alternative at this point.

Once seated, the waitress, who presumably had drawn the shortest straw, came over to take her order. "Coffee?" the waitress asked.

Her tag said Bonnie. "Why yes, Bonnie," said Maggie. "And the grand slam breakfast."

Bonnie hurried off, looking as though she had just risked her life. Maggie chuckled. *You're not too far from where I am, sister*, she thought. *None of you are.*

When her coffee came, she savored the smell and the warmth she felt as the liquid ran down her throat. Did other people appreciate this as much as she did? she wondered. *That was a benefit of deprivation*, she thought. *You really appreciated the simple things when you had access to them.*

As she rested, enjoying the warmth of the room and the coffee, she became aware of two men and a young woman sitting toward the back of the restaurant as well. They weren't as far back as she was, but they clearly wanted privacy. They spoke softly and in Spanish, which Maggie just happened to understand from one of her stops along the foster care highway. Another benefit of being homeless was that you were invisible.

"When will this take place?" the man with the stocking cap and nose ring asked.

"Valentine's Day, around dinnertime. I'd say six thirty

will catch people after work," the man with the leather jacket and hand tattoos, sitting next to the woman, answered.

"OK. How?" stocking cap man asked.

"Rooftops seem to be logical. It makes for an easy exit when it's done," said the tattoo man in the leather coat.

"Where?" stocking cap asked.

"North, just past Devon on Sheridan Road, in the crowded restaurant area. Our goal is to impact between twenty-five and thirty people," leather man replied.

"How many shooters do you prefer?" stocking cap man asked.

"That's up to you," said leather man. "You know the impact we're going for."

"Fee will be $250,000," said stocking cap man matter-of-factly.

"It will be transferred to you following the job," said leather jacket man.

"Great. Got it," said stocking cap man.

The woman they were with complained that she was hungry and couldn't wait any longer to eat. They all turned their attention to the menu and ordered when the waitress passed their table, after dropping off Maggie's food.

As Maggie ate her food, savoring every bite to prolong her indoor time, she thought about the conversation. Could this be the gang activity Helen had mentioned? Could she really save a few lives today? Whether it was that exact event or something else, there was certainly something big going down; $250,000 was no small change.

Now the question was whether she should stick her neck out for a city full of people who didn't know she existed and who couldn't care less if she froze to death on the street overnight.

But somewhere, deep inside, she felt as though she might have this one chance in her life to do something that was important. This might be her one shot at the rate she was going. She, if no one else, would know, and Helen would know, and that might be her only real contribution during this earthly life. The thing about Helen was that she was a Girl Scout. She believed in her clients. *Even in me*, she thought, and God only knew why. It sounded as if lives might be saved if she said something. She decided to get a hold of Helen. Unfortunately, she and her cell phone buddy had parted ways, meaning she'd need to find another way to contact Helen.

When her meal was gone, as in, everything on her plate was completely gone, she went into the restroom where she washed her face and armpits and wiped herself with a wet, soapy hand towel after using the facilities. *This is about the best it's going to get*, she thought. It was time for her to go back out into the elements, and she wasn't looking forward to it. Now, where was the closest library? She needed to send an email.

CHAPTER 18

Helen was at her desk. She was trying to reach Marty at the number he'd given her. After several rings, a pleasant female voice said hello.

"Hi. This is Helen Wagers. I'm calling for Marty. Is this his phone?" she asked.

"Oh, hi, Helen. It's Emma. Marty doesn't have a phone of his own. We have a house phone. I'll get him. He has news! He'll be excited to talk to you," Emma said.

Hmm. I wonder what's up, Helen thought.

"Hi, Helen!" Marty said, with an excited tone. "You'll never guess what's happened. It's so cool!"

"Really? I love cool news! Bring it!" she said. She almost never—no, wait, *never*—had started a client call with good news from the client.

"Zachary and I sold a song to U2 for $30,000 plus royalties. You'll need to buy their new album when it comes out in a year or so. I'll take you to lunch with my royalties," said Marty.

Helen didn't know if this was a joke or Marty was serious. "Tell me how it happened," she said.

Marty relayed the phone call and about talking to Bono and Zachary knowing how much to price the song and the legal documents being drawn up and how it was the most exciting day of his life—so far. He had hope. She could tell.

"I can't believe it!" Helen said. "I know someone who has talked to Bono in person, or on the phone at least. This is so cool, Marty. I'm so happy for you."

"In fact," she continued, "I was wondering if I might stop by the house on Friday again to check in with you and see how you're doing, although it sounds like you're doing better than I am," she joked, sort of.

"Sure, that would be great. But this time, you should come for dinner. It's an experience, believe me," Marty said, still elated.

"Well, if that's OK with Frances and everyone else, I'd love to do that," she replied sincerely. "Do you want to check with them and get back to me?"

"Nope," Marty replied. "I have no doubt. We eat at six o'clock. If you come a bit early, you can join us in the living room for a while. We usually gather there to get the chatting going before dinner and then continue it through and after dinner, but you've been there for that part before."

"I'll be there. And congratulations again, Marty. I'm so excited for you. See you Friday." The call ended. She sat at her desk for about fifteen minutes, trying to assimilate what she'd just heard. She kept reviewing it. "So Bono called the house to buy Marty's and Zachary's new song for his upcoming album." Then she'd repeat it again, like a mantra, only changing the wording sometimes to say, "My client Marty sold a song to U2. He was in a gang and addicted to heroin before being arrested twice, and now he's sold a song to U2." Maybe her Pollyanna-ism was manifesting in her clients?

Helen walked down to Chipotle around eleven thirty, hoping to avoid the crowd. She felt like getting out of the office and into the sunshine for a bit. It was bitter cold, and the dirty snow piles still lined the streets, but the sun was able to get through between the buildings, and that was what she needed.

She ordered carry-out food and headed back to the office with it. At her desk again, she checked her email while eating her salad. She noticed an email from daxYOU@gmail.com. Could that possibly be Maggie? Or was it spam. She opened it, and it turned out to be an authentic email from Maggie Dax. It was beautifully written, perfect grammar, syntax, everything. This was a truly smart woman, Helen lamented to herself.

The email read, "Helen, I overheard something this morning related to a topic you brought up during our last phone conversation. I'd like to share it with you privately if possible. If I overheard this, someone could easily overhear us, and I don't want to get caught in the middle of something like this. I'm up north at the Edgewater Branch of the library. I'll probably be able to hang around here for another hour or two before they hustle me out. I don't know if I can receive email on this public computer, so if I don't hear from you, I'll know you didn't get this, and I'll reach out again tomorrow."

Choking down her last bite of salad, Helen ran to the restroom, threw on her coat, and headed for the elevator. As she passed Tom's office, she saw that he was on a call. She didn't want to disturb him but grabbed a sticky note from his desk and wrote, "I may have a lead from Maggie re the gang stuff." He was turned toward his window, talking, so she just stuck it on the desk and headed for the exit.

She retrieved the ever-reliable Edith and headed north into midday traffic.

While she was new to this game, Helen wasn't laboring under any delusions. It was entirely possible that Maggie was tired of being cold and wanted to sit in Helen's car for a while and maybe get something to eat. Either way, whether Maggie had information or just wanted to hang out, it was an opportunity for further connection, and that was OK with her.

Helen entered the alley on the north side of the library and turned into the parking lot. Once inside, she headed for the bank of computers. She scanned the users but didn't spot Maggie until she heard her voice behind her saying, "Well, hi there, Cinderella. Want to take a ride in your car?"

"Sure," said Helen. "Let's go." And they headed out. First things first; they drove through Dunkin' Donuts for coffee and doughnut holes and then headed to a side street to park the car and talk.

"Thank you, Maggie," Helen said. "I appreciate this." She said it knowing Maggie's email could have been a bullshit excuse to get some free coffee and doughnuts, but hope springs eternal, and here they were.

"Yep," Maggie said. "I'm not used to being on the good guys' side of things, but it was too coincidental to have overhead what I did so shortly after you brought up gang stuff to me." And she relayed to Helen what she'd heard.

It was 2:00 p.m. when they finished talking, and Helen asked Maggie if she'd be willing to come back to the office with her to share this directly with her boss.

"Well, I have a lot on my plate, but if there's heat, indoor plumbing, and coffee, I'd be willing to juggle my schedule," she replied.

"Great," Helen said. "Let me call Tom to let him know we're on our way."

"Tom!" Maggie said. "I love Tom. I drove Tom crazy. That's when I was a bit younger and still had a lot of energy."

"Then he'll be thrilled to see you," Helen replied with a smirk, and they headed back downtown.

∘⋆∶•

Once in the office, Helen headed to the kitchen for hot chocolate for Maggie, her special request. It was 3:00 p.m., and they waited for Tom in the conference room. At 3:15, Tom came into the room and greeted Maggie. They obviously knew each other well.

Maggie began to relay what she'd heard as Tom and Maggie took notes.

3 individuals, 2 male, 1 female, Spanish-speaking
Aged between 20 and 40
Tattoos on hands
Nose ring
Meeting on North Side at Morning Mouth Breakfast Café
Young woman was companion of guy wearing leather jacket
Valentine's Day
Rooftops

Restaurant district just north of Devon on Sheridan
$250,000
Goal of 25–30 victims

These were all great details, and they'd relay them immediately to the detectives who'd asked for their help; however, the facts didn't explain why something was going to happen or who was involved. Gangs didn't typically plan random acts of chaos for no reason. Their activities were tied to their business enterprises, and the underlying purpose of this activity was not evident through these details.

Nevertheless, this information would hopefully help to save some lives and allay some terrible violence. They were all excited to contribute to that. Maggie seemed to be pleased with herself as well. Although she was still Maggie with the "Maggie edge."

"So, Tom, I'll bet you've missed me?"

"Well," Tom responded as he gathered his papers, "I would if I didn't see your name with some new infraction every twelve to fifteen months. Come on, Maggie. Aren't you tired of living like this? You're too smart. Why don't you let us help you get settled into something that will give you an easier life?"

"Old dog, new tricks, Tom. You know how it is," she said.

Once Tom left the room, Maggie asked to visit the restroom to get herself ready for a night on the streets. Maybe she'd try the women's shelter tonight. It was always kind of hit or miss, depending on the length of the line and the time you got into the line. With the temperature dropping below zero tonight, she imagined the line would be very long.

She came back to Helen's cube as Helen was packing up for the day. "Where can I drop you tonight, Mag?" Helen asked.

"How about driving me by the women's shelter on Diversey," Maggie replied. Helen knew that meant Maggie had nowhere to go in this frigid weather, and she decided to violate her own good sense by offering to get her a hotel room for the night. At least she'd be safe and get a decent night's sleep for one night. On the way there, she'd try to discuss a more permanent living situation with her—and a job to support it.

"I could do that, Maggie, but I think the line will be long tonight. Let's see if we can get you a room at the Holiday Inn near there, my treat. I can't afford this every night, but I'm hoping you'll like it so much you'll work with me to get a permanent room at a boarding house and a job at a fast-food place to pay the rent. You can't live the rest of your life roaming around in the freezing cold, hoping someone either rescues you or kills you. It doesn't make sense, Maggie. Please, think about it, and I'll come by the hotel in the morning. We can talk while you eat at the buffet, and then I'll bring you back to the office for your meeting with the city detectives in the morning."

Maggie looked surprised. She truly had not expected an offer like this. "Why are you offering this, Helen? Because I just gave you some information?"

Helen hesitated. "I'm sorry, Maggie. I hadn't even considered that. I was concerned about you being on the street looking for shelter all night. If I were not concerned about that, I wouldn't be in this job, believe me. It was great that you contacted me and offered what you'd overheard to us, but I looked at it more as a way for us to spend some time together. What you heard could have been worthless. I'm glad it wasn't, but it could have been. I truly don't believe you have to live the way you have been living, Maggie. All of us in the office feel like you are a very smart person with huge potential, who could do whatever she wanted to do if she'd only choose to. I'm here to help you get started. Let me do my job and help."

Maggie looked out the window at the people rushing around to get out of the cold. They all had a place to go to do that. Helen, like so many others before her, was telling Maggie that she, too, could have a place to go. Maggie tried to imagine that. She would continue to try to imagine that as she took a long bath tonight in a nice hotel room. She might even wash her clothes in the bathtub with the shampoo they provided in the room. It would be nice to be clean for a day.

Helen got Maggie checked into her room. The front desk person, who was new to the job, was a bit wary but couldn't turn down real money. The idea, as it had been explained to him, was that they rented rooms in exchange for money. He didn't know of anything else to do, although this person looked like a street person to him, smelled like stale smoke, and had no luggage. Hopefully she wouldn't trash the room, but if she did, he had the other young lady's credit card, so he couldn't get into that much trouble. "Enjoy your stay and call the front desk if you've forgotten any of the essentials, ma'am," he said.

"Oh, let's go ahead right now and load up on those essentials," Maggie answered. The desk clerk handed her a small cellophane bag with deodorant, a comb, a razor, a toothbrush, and toothpaste. Maggie was clearly elated. She grabbed two apples from the bowl and two chocolate chip cookies from the platter on the front desk and headed up to her room.

Helen thought, *What some people forget, others don't have.* She shouldn't have spent the money and violated common sense and every other rule caseworkers were supposed to follow. But she was glad she had.

Helen headed home.

CHAPTER 19

The next morning, Helen brought Maggie some clean clothes and a ski jacket she had bought for a trip she and Ryan had taken to Breckenridge in college. She and Maggie were both petite, and the clothes not only fit, but with Maggie's spa evening at the hotel, and a haircut that would be their next stop on the way to the office, another gift from Helen, no one would guess how Maggie lived from day to day.

While watching Maggie nosh on one of the everything from the complimentary buffet, as she stuffed her pockets with food for later, Hellen suggested that Maggie consider taking a job at one of the fast-food places Helen's department had a relationship with. They were attuned to working with people who were getting back on their feet, and with Maggie's innate intelligence, she'd have no problem getting up to speed.

There were lodgings near the few restaurants Helen had in mind, where Maggie could lease a room by the week until she had some money saved. They weren't in the greatest neighborhood, but with Maggie's experience, she'd be able to navigate the neighborhood until she was established enough to rent something.

Maggie listened as she ate but didn't comment. Then she took the clothes Helen had brought, went up to her room, changed, and they checked out. Edith took them to a local Fast Cuts where Maggie's hair was cut in a cute bob style, after which they headed to the office where the detectives wanted to debrief Maggie.

Helen went to her cubicle to get some work done while the police talked with Maggie. It had been interesting to see Tom's reaction when he entered the conference room and saw Maggie. He did a double take, to say the least, and Maggie noticed it. Maggie noticed everything.

●ᵜ˙ *

It was finally Friday, and Helen was surprised by an early call from Ryan.

"Hey, sorry to call so early. Just wanted you to know a bunch of us are getting together tonight after work at Embellish. Everyone has been asking about you. We're planning to be there by six," he said as impartially as he could.

"Oh. Wow. Good morning," Helen said groggily. She was halfway through a cup of coffee, sitting in the living room of her flat, staring out a window at the street. She hadn't contemplated speaking out loud until she got to work, so she sounded barely conscious, she was sure.

"I would love to see everyone, of course, but I'll be out at that client's house I was at the weekend before the big snowstorm. I'm having dinner with their little community, so not sure what time I'd get there," she said sincerely.

"Well, we'll probably be there until we break up for dinner. I can text you the restaurant where we end up if that will help. You could just visit with everyone while we all eat," Ryan said hopefully.

"I'll try, Ryan. But if the timing doesn't work, please let me know when you're all getting together again. I'd love to see everybody," Helen said, hoping he knew that "everybody" included him.

"Great then," he said. "Nice to hear your voice, Lennie."

"Likewise, Ryan," she said. "And thanks for thinking of me." And they ended the call.

She realized she was looking forward to dinner at the house. She had some business to accomplish with Marty while there. It was time for his monthly blood test. He was going to need to make a trip out of the house to get to Stroger Hospital Clinic, and she hoped they could come up with a plan for him to do that without the temptations of the street or the threats of his former gang members.

Once at work, her day progressed as expected. She had meetings, phone calls, emails, and lunch and then headed out to drive around to check in with various clients.

She had succeeded in talking Maggie into a temporary living situation for the next week or so. She could stay longer than a week, if she would, and Helen hoped she would. She hoped Maggie liked being clean, warm, and well fed enough to choose to stay. She had also talked Maggie into meeting with the owner of a fast-food franchise who had a rocky youth himself and supported their efforts to get young people like himself into the workforce.

She had to let that one play itself out. Her focus today

was on Marty. She headed toward the house around four o'clock, knowing that Friday-afternoon traffic might be bad, as it turned out to be.

Around 5:15 p.m., she exited the parking lot. She drove around a bit, trying to remember where the hidden road was, until she finally found it at five thirty on the dot. She was looking forward to the gathering in the living room to see how Marty was doing but also just being in the company of such a chill group of talented people. It did her heart good after having spent the week chasing around people who seemed determined to create chaos for themselves and others.

She knocked on the front door this time.

Marty greeted her at the door and welcomed her into the foyer, where he took her coat and gave her a big hug. He led her into the living room, where everyone except Frances was drinking tea and catching up on the day and the week. At about 5:45, Donald excused himself to check on Frances and lend her a hand.

The room was electric with energy from the young people. Marty and Zachary's news about U2 and their song was the highlight of the conversation, initially. But then Marty turned to Emma and Angela, saying, "And in other news, these two have succeeded in getting live auditions for Emma for two stage plays that will open in Chicago next fall, and a Netflix series that will shoot here this summer!"

"Wow!" Helen exclaimed. "Tell me how you did that."

Angela explained having researched the various theatre companies in the city that Emma had identified. Those companies had been auditioning by putting out scripts and character descriptions and asking actors to submit files with their audition, along with résumés and references. This had worked for them during COVID, and they apparently didn't see a reason to go back to in-person auditions until they got closer to make the final casting decisions, at which time they'd need to see actors together to understand chemistry, stage presence, voice tone in a theatre setting, and all those things they could only accomplish live.

In the meantime, Angela, using a new computer with a new IP address, as well as new email and company name, had secured several bids to do coding for companies that were jobbing out IT projects. She had underbid everyone initially, which she was able to do because she was living free of charge now. The idea was to build a résumé with good references on her site, after which she'd charge market rates and be able to contribute to the household.

It was all amazing to Helen. These people, having come from a variety of hardships, were flourishing in a way that she had only hoped could be. This was what Maggie would call her Girl Scout mentality come to life. She wished she could tell Maggie about it. And Tom. And everyone else in America. But that probably wasn't prudent at the present time.

The bell rang from the kitchen, and the cows headed in from the pasture. Or that's what it felt like anyway. Everyone knew there was something amazing on that buffet, and they couldn't wait to see, smell, and taste it.

Frances approached Helen as everyone took their seats. After a quick hug, she led her to a seat next to her own at the head of the table. Tonight, the dinner was plated. It was beef tenderloin with crab meat garnish and a cube of potato au gratin, next to a beautiful stem of broccoli. And homemade bread, of course.

Everyone bowed their heads to give thanks. They then tried to casually take up their forks and knives, but their exuberance was difficult to contain. Finally, Zachary said, "Geez, Frances." And after that, there was no conversation for a bit while they all savored the beautiful meal, lovingly prepared and elegantly presented.

Frances served coffee afterward, and a large scoop of raspberry trifle for each person. When she was seated, she began the conversation by thanking Helen for being their guest. "I had to prepare something a little special for our special guest, Helen."

Helen thanked her profusely, saying, "I feel like there are so many wonderful things happening in this house. It's exciting to hear everyone's news. It's all amazing, and I feel like I'm privileged to know about it."

"Well, we appreciate what you do for Marty, dear. He means the world to us. And tell us about your week, Helen. You have such an interesting job and meet so many unique people."

Unique, thought Helen. *I guess that's one way to look at it.*

"I did have some excitement this week," Helen said. "We have been aware that the gangs have something planned in the city this winter but didn't have any insight into what it would be, who would be affected, and so on.

"The detectives who work on gang crime in the city asked us to run it by our clients to see if they were hearing anything on the street. And one of my clients, an amazing young woman named Maggie, happened to overhear a conversation about a crime being planned on Valentine's Day on the North Side. In fact, it's on a scale of a terrorist attack in my mind. Really sick," Helen said with disgust.

"Really?" asked Marty. "I wonder if my old gang is involved. I could help you if they are."

Helen turned to Marty, saying, "No, Marty. I wouldn't jeopardize everything you've accomplished to get away from them by letting you do that. No."

"But, Helen," he said, "I do have to go to Stroger. And you know they wait around there every day. I could talk to them. Maybe they'd open up to me. Especially if they're recruiting for some big event."

While everyone around the table watched and listened, Helen rejected the idea. "Talking to gang members, where the drugs and temptation came from in the first place, seems imprudent, Marty. No."

With that, Emma and Marty began collecting dinnerware. Frances invited everyone back into the living room, where they poured another cup of coffee and settled in front of the fire.

"Helen," Frances said once they were all seated, "not to sound like a helicopter parent, but we're all wondering how to get Marty to and from the hospital safely for his bloodwork. Do you have any ideas? Would he be safer if he took an Uber or if one of us drove him? Or is there some other way?"

Helen thought for a moment. "I guess I could pick him up from the train when it gets into the city and take him to the hospital clinic in the morning. There isn't a good way to get into the city on a weekday, other than by train. It's a tough thing to plan around. The problem is that the blood test is kind of like going to the emergency room—meaning you check in, and then you sit and wait until it's your turn. And if there's a shooting or an accident, everyone just waits and waits. It can be a very long day, so it's difficult to know when Marty would be finished and need to get back to the train. In certain instances, they've told our clients to come back the next day, because of the chaos they deal with at that hospital."

"We'll talk about it among ourselves and figure something out. It is paramount to all of us that Marty be safe," Frances said.

When Marty and Emma entered the room, having taken care of the dinner dishes, Frances asked Marty and Zachary to play their U2 song for them. They did, and it was as great as Bono had said. Then they sped it up and got it more *U2ey* to give everyone an idea of what the band might do with it. It was a great evening of fun, music, laughter, and positivity in general.

As Helen thanked Frances again, told Marty she'd talk with him early the next week, and said her goodbyes to the other residents, she was once again struck by the difference in this place compared to the outside world. There seemed to be contentment, creativity, and goodwill. She knew it all had to do with Frances, but she didn't understand if it was just a gift she had or if there was a bit more to it than just Frances's personality. Something to continue to ponder.

Helen found the last parking spot on her block, at the corner, and hoped the inches that Edith extended beyond the "No Parking Here to Corner" sign would not garner her the dreaded Chicago parking ticket, a truly nefarious thing. It wasn't until she had gathered her laptop, briefcase, scarf, gloves, and purse that she realized she'd completely forgotten about Ryan's invitation to meet everyone this evening.

She stumbled up the stairs, dropped everything, took off her boots, found her keys in her pocket, and practically fell in the door, where her roommates sat around the TV with glasses of wine, watching reruns of *The Office*. She checked her phone, and sure enough, Ryan had texted her. They were at Elephant and Castle in the Loop, and it would be loud with playoff games blaring. She knew she wouldn't be able to talk with anyone in that environment anyway. She'd just call Lilly tomorrow and get all the news from the evening. She needed to get together with Lilly, maybe sometime this weekend.

She texted Ryan, letting him know that she'd just now gotten out of work and thanking him for keeping her "in the loop," no pun intended. "I hope I see everyone soon," she concluded.

⁂

Helen spent the weekend doing laundry, buying groceries, napping, writing reports for work, and cleaning the apartment, and on Sunday morning, she met Lilly for coffee and scones at Sip of Hope in the Logan Square neighborhood of Chicago.

"We missed you on Friday, Lennie," Lilly said as she sat

down with her cappuccino and blueberry scone. Helen had already started on her muffin and latte.

"I missed you guys too," she said. She did miss them. She couldn't seem to see any of them with her crazy schedule, but she did have close friendships with many of them, extending back to their days in college.

"So what's up with you and Ryan?" Lilly asked. "He seems lost and confused."

"Well, we're taking a break, Lill. It was time. We're not in college anymore. We have adult jobs and responsibilities. I got home from work close to nine on Friday night. All I wanted to do was go back to my apartment and hang out for a while with my roommates before going to sleep.

"I know Ryan doesn't understand. I really do think it's because of the difference between our jobs and how we spend our days," she finished, hoping Lilly might offer her some empathy.

"I know he doesn't understand too. He can't figure out why you don't get a job that has regular hours so you can have a life," Lilly said. "I really believe he thought you two were settled and would be together for good."

"I thought that too, Lill; all the more reason to take this break and make sure we are right for each other. I don't want to live like I'm still in college. And even if I wanted to, there's no way with my job that I can," Helen said.

"I wish you'd get over the idea of saving the world, Lennie," Lilly said. "I know that if anyone can do it, it's you. But it's just too grown-up. Where's the fun?

"Well, whatever. We all have to do what we have to do. I just hope it all makes you happy in the end. Ryan is a great guy, and he adores you. If you lose him, will you regret it? I'd love to have a Ryan to settle down with," Lilly mused while munching.

"Someone amazing will come along when you're ready," Helen assured her. "Until then, do what you want to do. These days are for us to figure out who we are."

Lilly shrugged, apparently not convinced, after which she began updating Helen on all their friends, what they were doing, how their jobs were going, who they were dating, where they were going on vacation, where they had rented an apartment, and more. They talked until Sip of Hope closed at noon, when they reluctantly headed their separate ways. Helen had truly missed Lilly and the rest of the group. She knew that. She still didn't know where they fit into her life these days though.

CHAPTER 20

On Monday morning, Helen got to work early. It was going to be another busy week. She was beginning the process of closing out certain clients whose periods of supervision had been fulfilled, while reviewing files for potential new clients to take their slots.

She got up to stretch her legs, visit the restroom, and get some coffee around midmorning. On her way back, she checked in with Tom, who wasn't on the phone, for once.

"How's it going?" he asked her.

"Good, I think," she said. "I have a client, Marty, who is doing so well it's overwhelming to me. I know it isn't because of me or anything I'm doing, so I can't take credit. I just wish I could bottle whatever it is.

"And then there's Maggie. She's agreed to stay at a place I got for her temporarily and to talk to Bennie Grimes about working at one of his franchise restaurants. I feel like maybe the world is ending or something," Helen concluded.

Tom laughed. "Keep these days in mind when everything seems to be going the other direction."

She headed back to her cube as her desk phone started

to ring. There was no name on the caller ID. It just said "unlisted."

"Helen Wagers," she answered.

"Hi, Helen. It's Frances. Is this a good time to talk, or could we schedule a time for a short chat?"

"My goodness, Frances," Helen said enthusiastically. "I'd love to chat."

"Great. Thank you, dear. Donald and I have been talking about ways to get Marty to and from the city safely for his blood test. Would it be possible for one of us to accompany him—that is, if he wanted that? I mean, is the hospital accommodating to family or friends accompanying patients?" Frances asked.

"I think so, but I'll need to check, Frances. Things have changed since COVID, and hospitals are still requiring certain protocols. I can contact the hospital and get back to you tomorrow," Helen said.

"That would be wonderful, dear," Frances said.

But it seemed that she had more to talk about, so Helen waited and then asked, "How is everything else going, Frances?"

"Well, dear, at the risk of sticking my nose into places it shouldn't be, I had two other items I wanted to discuss with you. The first is about a connection I have with a private investigation firm. They work out of multiple cities and might be able to offer some insight into your question about an upcoming gang activity. If they had come across something in the course of their work, there would be no charge for them to share with you what they were hearing. I would just need to ask," said Frances, in her calm, lovely way.

"My question is, would you like me to ask?"

"I think that would be amazing, Frances! And I know my supervisor and the detectives working in the gang crime unit in the city would be super grateful," Helen answered enthusiastically.

"That's the thing, though, dear," Frances said gently. "I don't think my friend would be interested in talking with all those official people. Too much publicity. Too many politics. My friend would tell me, and I would pass it along to you. How you explained the origin of that information when you shared it with them would be up to you."

"Oh, OK," Helen answered. She didn't want to turn down information, regardless of where it was coming from. So she just left it at that.

"And lastly," Frances said, "and please feel free to tell me if I'm out of line, I was interested to learn more about the young woman you mentioned when you were here on Friday. I think her name was Maggie? You said she was amazing. It piqued my interest."

"Yes, her name is Maggie, and I do think of her as an amazing girl, Frances, although many of my colleagues break out in a rash when they remember dealing with her." Helen chuckled. "She is extremely bright and has amazing street smarts. She had a difficult upbringing and a lot of emotional baggage with her. She's only twenty-two years old but has been in and out of the system since her early teens. I'd say if it could be tried, she's tried it. And yet she's survived.

"She is the one who brought us the information we have about gang activity. She overheard it in a café. The truly amazing thing about it is that she came to us with that information. She doesn't fancy herself as a part of the establishment, so she is, as she says, working for the good guys, which is not where she typically sees herself," Helen said.

"I'm hoping it is the beginning of something good for her—that she is interacting with me and allowing me to help her get cleaned up and off the streets during these freezing cold months. She'll be off my client list this coming month, and I kind of hate to see her go now. I'd like to see if we could continue to make progress."

"Hmmm," Frances said. "Well, I'm happy to hear that, Helen. You seem to have a very good effect on the clients you work with. I know Marty respects you, and it motivates him to want to make you proud. Maybe you're having the same effect on Maggie. I certainly hope so.

"I will await your call tomorrow, and if possible, one of us will accompany Marty for his blood test," Frances concluded.

"Thank you so much, Frances," Helen replied. "I am grateful to you and your community for your support of him."

CHAPTER 21

Frances remained in the office at the house and made another call.

"Hello, Parker. It's Frances. How are you today?"

"Always happy when I'm talking to you, Frannie. How can I help?" Parker Bennett replied.

"I wanted to check in with you regarding Rooney and his activities, as well as to run a new situation by you," Frances said, getting right to business.

Parker Bennett and Frances Miller went way back, as they say. Parker was the son of another family Frances had been raised with. He was Ivy League educated and would have been running his family's corporate investments overseas had he not enlisted in the army at the time of Desert Storm. It would be difficult to describe the horror on his mother's face and the color of his father's complexion when he shared with them what he'd done. He was in his mid-twenties at the time and working with the family business. This seemed to come out of the blue.

His instincts must have been correct though. It became apparent after a few years that he had a gift for special clandestine operations. After 9/11, he was sent to Afghanistan, where he helped to uncover and destroy Al-Qaeda.

In fact, he'd only returned to the States when it was clear that he could no longer endure the privations of undercover work at his age. His family had sold their interest in the business they had started, and he was mulling over options when Frances learned he was back in the States. She talked to him about going into business together. She and he both had venture capital from their respective holdings. The only business Parker felt qualified to run was investigation. Frances supported him because she knew he was honest, sincere, and highly skilled. The result had been branches of their firm, called BenMil, in the northern, southern, eastern and western regions of the US.

"Let's start with Rooney," Parker said. "That guy is scum, Frannie. It's a good thing your young friend got away from him when she did. I'm sure he's desperate to find her, and the IT protections we worked on with her should keep her safe. Just don't let her go walking around his neighborhood or meeting friends or family there. He's a bad dude."

"Oh, she won't. Is there any chance he will be off the streets in the future? That would allow her—Angela is her name—to have a more normal life," Frances asked.

"I hope so. We're working on it. Compared to the truly big players, he would be considered an amateur. The problem is he's made some money doing something illegal, and he thinks he's big-time. I won't burden you with all the details, but just be assured that he's on our radar now, and we'll keep an eye on him," said Parker. "And there's more?"

"Yes, this is broader I would think. One of my 'family' members here is still under supervision. His caseworker is a lovely girl; Helen is her name. She is so sincere and focused on her clients. Anyway, she came out to the house for dinner with us last week and talked about some large-scale gang event that Chicago detectives are aware of but about which they know almost nothing.

"Then, last week, another of Helen's clients overheard a conversation between two men in a café. The men spoke in Spanish about doing something from a rooftop in a neighborhood to the far north in the city. They mentioned Valentine's Day at the dinner hour, so they are talking about crowded streets.

"The question that's still out there is why? What is the underlying purpose? And why are they doing this on Valentine's Day?" Frances said.

"I talked to Helen before this call," Frances continued. "I said I had a special relationship with a private investigation firm and would be willing to ask if they had heard anything while investigating their various other jobs. She thought that would be good. I also told her I'd relay anything I learned to her directly and did not want to get involved with the city officials in any way."

"That's great," Parker said. "Nothing positive could come from getting tangled up with their political power struggles."

"What is positive is that the detectives are now aware of this rooftop event and can hopefully stop it. However,

Helen says the bad thing is that they have no context. As in, is this an isolated event or will it be citywide? Is it a vendetta against some business owner in the area? Or is it gangland war for the sake of turf? And I'll stop there, Parker, because, as you can tell, I am now delving into crime novels I've read for ideas," Frances concluded.

"And I can tell you paid attention to those plotlines, Frannie," he said, and they both chuckled. "We'll check into it and see what we can find."

"Thank you, dearest. Be safe," said Frances.

"Of course, always," replied Parker.

CHAPTER 22

Helen was assured that each patient at the Stroger Clinic could be accompanied by one adult. She called the house to let Frances know. Donald answered. It was midmorning, and she could hear the faint sound of music in the background, meaning Marty and Zachary were busy at work.

"Hello, Helen!" Donald said when she identified herself. "How are you doing this brisk winter morning? It's Donald."

"Hi, Donald. All is well. Just wanted to let Frances know that the hospital allows one companion per patient, so if Marty is up for it, he may bring someone with him for his lab appointment.

"Terrific!" Donald replied, truly pleased. I'll relay the news to Frances when she returns from errands. "We shall discuss his preference at dinner. If he would like company, he shall have it. And have a wonderful day, Helen."

"Thank you, Donald."

Zachary volunteered to accompany Marty. His rationale was sound.

"Hell," Zachary had said, "if something happens to you, Marty, my newfound fame will be so short-lived I'll be a one-hit wonder! It'll be Bono and then nothing. I think I should go with you, and we'll be in this together, just like we're in business together."

Marty was truly touched by their concern and their vigilance on his behalf. To say that no one had really had his back since he was a little child would not be an exaggeration. It felt so good to have family around him again.

"I am really touched by your outpouring of concern. Thank you for your support. And, yes, Zachary, I would welcome your company tomorrow. Let's take the early train and try to get in and out as quickly as possible."

"Got it!" Zachary replied. "And thanks for accommodating us, bro. We want you to be safe, and I want you to write more songs for me!"

Everyone chuckled, and Zachary and Angela cleared the table and got the kitchen cleaned and in order. Then they all migrated to the parlor for some music. A special treat tonight was Emma's most recent audition tape, which Angela showed on the smart TV. It was really very good. Emma had a connection to the camera and the audience that was innate. There was no telling where it could take her.

Everyone retired to their own rooms early, around nine o'clock. Tomorrow would be an early day for Frances, who would drive Marty and Zachary to the parking lot to catch the 6:00 a.m. train.

CHAPTER 23

Parker Bennett met with his executive team via Zoom midweek and brought them up to speed on his call with Frances. Their first subject was Rooney Hardy.

"As you know, sex trafficking across the border from El Paso, Texas, is generating as much as fourteen million dollars a month for the stakeholders who are transporting these people," Parker began.

"It appears that this Rooney character met up with some Latinos in Chicago who brought him in on a trafficking deal in which he made a pretty penny for a local boy. By using his little company to launder money, they allowed him to benefit from the proceeds, which, probably unbeknownst to him, were hundreds of thousands more lucrative than his little cut. Nevertheless, it was huge money to him, and he expressed interest in continuing the collaboration.

"A few months ago, when his girlfriend, Angela McCall, found refuge at Frances's house, she did so because he had been exceedingly agitated the evening prior at a restaurant where they were supposed to have had dinner. She thought she may have met with a man in the bathroom, after which he was in a rage and insisted they go home. The next morning, he had flown to Texas unexpectedly."

Guy Padilla, from the southern region of BenMil, Ltd., continued, "We went back to check on his activities in Texas that morning. He had headed straight toward the El Paso border when his flight landed. He apparently believed he had been double-crossed in an upcoming deal. Who knows what he thought he was going to do, or to whom, when he arrived, but it was probably the luckiest day of his life, because there had been a huge bust, and a semi filled with young women and girls had been found. The area was full of emergency vehicles and police, so Hardy turned tail and ran back to the airport. He returned home that same evening."

"And ever since that time," Parker chimed in, "he's been on the hunt for Angela, the girlfriend who is now safe with Frances, while at the same time trying to keep his foot in with the guys he did the first deal with."

"What's interesting though is that those guys don't want anything to do with a hothead," said Patty Daly, whose responsibility for BenMil was the central states area. "They've been giving him the runaround, and he's getting meaner and meaner as a result.

"In addition, we're looking into one more thing, just to get the bigger picture," Patty said. "Angela mentioned to Frances a prior girlfriend of his named Charlotte. We've been looking everywhere for Charlotte, but to no avail at this point. We will continue to search though."

"Great. Thank you, Patty and Guy," Parker said. "Now, there's new work that I'd like to brief you on. This may cross territories or may be a Chicago local thing, but I want to keep our minds open to either possibility at this point.

"There's something going on with the gangs in Chicago, and they're pulling out some of their big guns, both literally and figuratively it seems.

"It seems the Chicago gangland detective squad," Parker continued, "has been observing some excitement on the street, which typically means there's something being planned. Oddly enough, one of Frances's contacts alluded to this. Frances has a resident at the house who is just winding up post-detention supervision. Frances has met his caseworker, and that young woman mentioned to Frances that she has been asked to talk with her clients about it, assuming they are closest to the street noise.

"Coincidentally, one of her clients did overhear a conversation in a breakfast café about a rooftop event above a crowded restaurant area on Valentine's Day. They know the location and so hopefully have that event covered. What lies beneath the surface is what we want to find out. Is there more to this than meets the eye?"

"And the source is reliable?" Guy asked. "Was it really a coincidence that he or she overheard this?"

"I think they believe the source, or at least feel it would be too dangerous *not* to believe the source, having no other hard information and knowing that something is up," Parker said.

"And so I think we must do the same," he continued. "We need to know what the underlying activity is, if there is underlying activity. We need to know who the drivers are and who the hired help is. We need to know what the merchandise is or the power objective.

"I'll go ahead and leave that with all of you, and we'll wind things up for now. We'll meet again in a week. With the February 14 date, we don't have much time to work on this. In fact, a matter of weeks. Let me know if I can do anything to facilitate your progress. In the meantime, I will ask to talk with the source in order to glean any additional details she may have," Parker concluded. "And thank you to all of you. I am grateful to have such a strong team to work with."

CHAPTER 24

Marty and Zachary met in the kitchen at 5:40 a.m. to catch the train from the parking lot into the city. Frances handed them each a paper cup filled with the elixir of life, and they headed out to the truck. It was freezing cold and dark. Next to the house on the highway, miles of red taillights headed into the city, trying to get a jump on true morning rush hour traffic that would lead to a standstill on the road in a half hour or so. It was otherworldly, really.

Once on the train, and having ingested enough coffee to emit sound, Zachary turned to Marty and said, "I must remember to give thanks, next time we bow our heads before dinner, that I'm not in one of those cars, day after day, at this hour of the morning."

"Ditto," Marty said. Or maybe he said something else, Zachary thought. It took Marty a lot of coffee to rev up in the morning.

Closer to the city, they had a front row seat to a multicar pileup near Racine. Zachary reiterated his gratitude. Maybe it was the hour of the day and maybe it was the need for more caffeine, but what they failed to realize was that this type of accident would be the very thing that would take precedent at Stroger, making it likely that their day would be long and tedious.

They got into the station, transferred to an El train, and arrived at the hospital around 8:00 a.m., only to find emergency vehicles all over the place. They were told to go around the building to the front entrance and to make their way to the clinic through the hospital, rather than through the outside entrance, which they did.

Marty checked in, and they found a seat. One TV was tuned to a home renovation network. The others to local and national news. The accident was displayed prominently on the local networks, with pictures of the backed-up traffic on the highway leading into the city from the south.

"Well, this is gonna take all day," Marty said.

"Yep," Zachary replied. "We should go get breakfast in the cafeteria." Zachary was a foodie. Even when the food was hospital food.

"You go," Marty said, "and bring me a muffin or something. I'm afraid to leave, just in case there is some kind of miracle, and they call me."

"OK," Zachary said, and headed toward the cafeteria.

Marty was working through a couple of tunes in his head, with his eyes closed, when he heard someone sit down next to him. He opened his eyes to glance sideways, hoping there'd be room for Zachary to sit when he came back.

"Hey, Marty. What's shakin'?" a familiar voice said.

It was Paolo, from Marty's old gang.

"I've been hoping to run into you one of these days," Paolo said. "The way I figure it, you're about at the end of your supervision and should be able to make a housing change. We're all hoping you'll be rejoining our little family. We can't wait to hear about the guys on the inside and what they're all talking about."

Marty had thought about this eventuality for a long time. He had seen guys from the gang every time he'd had bloodwork since he'd been released. And with Helen's recent query over the gangs and their activities, he wondered if there would be a way for him to learn anything during one of these visits.

"Yeah, I'm good, Paolo. Everybody OK at home base?"

"Sure. Why don't you come by and visit sometime soon? We'd be happy to bring you up to date on current business activities. Lots of exciting stuff is coming up. You'd really like to be a part of it. Good money. And some of those party favors you're so fond of as well," Paolo said, talking about heroin, which had been Marty's drug of choice.

"I'll certainly consider that and look for an opportunity, Paolo. I'm watched pretty good right now, man, but I'll look for an opening," Marty said.

"Great," Paolo replied. "I'll tell Sammy to look for you and that you want to know more about this new deal. We need some experienced guys, so he'd like to have you."

"Good seein' you, man," Marty said. "Take care."

Zachary came back just around the time Paolo was getting up. "Were you talking to that guy?" Zachary asked.

"I was," said Marty. "An old acquaintance."

"Everything OK?" Zachary asked as he handed Marty more coffee and a muffin.

"Marty Munos," a phlebotomist called from the

doorway. Thrilled about the early call and dismayed about handing his coffee and muffin to Zachary, Marty proceeded to the doorway and disappeared with the nurse. He returned ten minutes later with a Snoopy bandage and asked Zachary to call an Uber on his burn phone. Marty thought he'd call Helen when he got home. She would be worried.

Once on the train, they texted Frances to let her know they were headed back to the house, and that all was well. She sounded elated and thanked Marty for his call.

Marty devoured his muffin like it was his first meal in a year. It was pretty good.

"Hey, Mart, who was that guy you were talking to in the waiting area at the hospital?" Zachary asked. "Did the gang guys get into that waiting area somehow? So much for hospital security."

"He was a member of my old gang," Marty replied. "And he confirmed that something big is coming up soon. They want me to come back and work with them on it. And there'll be heroin for me if I do," he said.

"Terrific. Well, at least they won't be able to get at you now," Zachary replied, trying to think of something positive to say, but in truth, worrying about next month's blood test when they had to do this again. "These gang guys must watch that hospital clinic pretty closely, eh?"

"Yep, they're on it. That's for sure," Marty replied. "I don't want to sound crazy or anything, Zach, but I'm wondering if there's a way I can get more information out of them for the detectives."

"Yep. That's crazy. What are you thinking? You are

so vulnerable! Stop!" Zachary was getting himself worked up now.

"I am vulnerable; that's a fact. I had a drug habit and hung around with people who murdered other people. It was all so bad," Marty acknowledged.

"Right, but no more, Mart. You're out of it. You're safe. You can have a life. Why would you risk all that?" Zachary asked.

"To repair some of the damage I've done," Marty replied. "It may be a terrible idea, but I'll talk to Frances and Donald and Helen about it openly. No sneaking around. I'm uniquely connected in a way most people can never be. They don't know which way I'm going once my supervision is over. Last time, I went back to them. They have reason to trust that I'll do it again. If I can get back in contact long enough to gather some intel about what's up on the street, I can bring it back, and the professionals can use it."

Zachary had a pained look on his face. And Marty knew it was sincere. Marty also knew it made sense for him to be concerned. They were silent for the rest of the trip.

At dinner that night, everyone was elated that the blood test outing had gone as smoothly as it had. Especially considering the shitshow the multicar pileup on the "Damn Ryan" expressway had created.

"Yep, the Force was with you guys," Emma said.

"Thank God for the Force," Angela added.

They had a cheerful evening with music and poetry, and

the day was happily concluded, with no apparent worries about tomorrow.

The next morning, they had their regular breakfast repast and headed off to their respective areas of the house to work. Marty, however, asked Frances and Donald if they had a minute to chat about an idea he had.

He shared his thoughts about the gang infiltration with them. They both looked distressed, which was a layer far beyond concerned.

"We respect your desire to contribute, young man, truly we do," said Donald.

"But we feel it's very early in your recovery to expose yourself to the risk you are contemplating," Frances said.

"I will, however, talk with my colleagues who are investigating this situation, while you talk to Helen, and we will meet again over this issue in a couple of days," Frances concluded. "Is that satisfactory?"

"Yes, thank you," Marty said, and headed off to the parlor, where Zachary was waiting to start working on several jingles they'd been asked to bid on for Lipton Tea.

CHAPTER 25

The following afternoon, the house phone rang. Donald arose from his well-worn perch in the library to answer it. "Good afternoon," he answered. It was Helen, asking for Frances.

"Just one moment, please," he said. "I believe she's in the kitchen concocting something amazing. I may need to relieve her."

She heard him set down the receiver, which was not a familiar sound to anyone from her generation. In a moment, Frances came to the phone.

"Hello, dear. I'm so happy to talk with you. I just left Donald in the kitchen, wearing a flowered apron I insisted he put on, and stirring a large pot of soup."

"Oh, Frances, I apologize," Helen said. "I didn't mean to pull you away from what you were doing. I just felt that you'd want to deal with this situation with Marty as soon as possible."

"As indeed I do, dear," Frances said, always gracious. "And believe me, it was worth it to see Donald in that apron. Go ahead. I'm listening."

"I talked with my boss, Tom, and he talked with the Chicago detectives who deal with gangland activity. They agree, because it's obvious, really, that Marty would be uniquely placed to infiltrate the gang hierarchy and find out what's going on. The question is whether that is the best thing for Marty. He has been clean from the heroin for eighteen months. He was an occasional user, and he told me that it came from the gang's stash, so it was pure and only given to him occasionally, so he couldn't have access to it randomly," Helen said, "which may have kept him from becoming a daily user. It also kept him tied to them.

"Which leads to my worst-case scenario fear, which is that they'd use it on him forcibly if they suspected he was not 100 percent under their control. For me to be supportive in any way of his interaction with this gang, I would have to believe he was safe at all times, as in, maybe a meeting with them in a public place to hear what they had in mind, and then back to safety under the pretense that he was going home to gather up his stuff to move back to them for good.

"In fact," Helen said, "maybe it could be tied somehow to his next blood test, which will be his last one under supervision."

Frances listened. She could tell Helen was very torn about Marty's safety, as was she. At the same time, she knew there could be a lot at stake and that Marty wanted to help.

Finally, she said, "Helen, I appreciate your apprehension. In fact, I share it. And I relayed that to my PI contact person, who is a lifelong friend and who I would trust with my life. I asked if he and his team could in any way guarantee Marty's safety if he interacted with these gang members to gather information.

"What he told me is that he believes his team would be able to be in the vicinity without detection and that they could create a diversion should they see things beginning to go awry. They would choreograph the interaction around Marty's next blood test, counting on the gang to approach Marty as they did this past time. I don't know any more than that," Frances said quietly.

"I see," Helen said. "What does your gut tell you, Frances?"

"My gut is churning," Frances said. "My inclination is to create a safe place for my family and never to compromise their safety. This is unsettling ground for me. I will have to trust in the vigilance of others and step out of the way if Marty chooses to pursue this.

"What does your gut tell you, Helen?"

"My boss, Tom, had a meeting with the city's detectives yesterday. He let me sit in. There are some very terrible things that could be happening as part of this gang stuff in the next few weeks. Lives could be lost in the event we know about up north, but beyond that, depending upon what their objective is, which could be a gang war over turf, a massive drug shipment, weapons, human trafficking, whatever, many lives could be destroyed," Helen replied.

"I went into this field to repair lives. I know I'm new to all this, but the thought of losing the progress Marty has made with you is devastating to me. The thought of hundreds of innocent people dying when we might have been able to stop it is also devastating to me," Helen mused.

"And finally, I wonder the impact it would have on Marty's self-esteem and self-image if we attempt to control him now, telling him he cannot do the brave thing he has proposed. Is it really our call?" Helen concluded.

"Donald and I will talk with Marty this evening," Frances concluded. "If he does want to proceed, I will propose the following: there will need to be a logistics plan developed by my PI contact. I only trust him. That plan can then be communicated to the detectives in complete confidence. My idea is that the detectives will benefit from the information gathered, but the collection of that information will be under the supervision of the PI team.

"You may want to run those conditions by your boss for conveyance to the detectives. If they are not supportive of those terms, I know Donald and I will not be supportive about the risk when we meet with Marty.

"Ultimately, of course, it is Marty's choice how he wants to manage all of this. It is his life," Frances concluded. "I will be talking with you daily for the rest of week I imagine, dear, so until tomorrow."

"Yes. And thank you so much, Frances. I really cannot imagine having this conversation or even considering this action with anyone but you," Helen said.

Helen looked at her cell phone after the call, only to find a text from Lilly. Everyone was getting together after work again at Embellish. Lilly wanted her to know, since it wasn't a Friday, and she might not have a conflict.

After that phone call with Frances, she thought, *some*

mindless conversation might be good for me. She wrapped things up, put her desk in order, put on her coat, and headed for the door.

As she passed Tom's office, she said, "Good night," and kept going. She didn't want to review her conversation with Frances with him right now. It was all too much to handle.

She picked up Edith and drove to Embellish a bit early, where she found Lilly and Ryan at the bar. They made space for her in between, and all began to talk about what was happening in their lives, in their friends' lives, in their roommates' lives, on their jobs, with their coworkers, with their former college roommates, their siblings, their parents, and their pets. As each friend came in, some with coworkers and roommates, new members of the group Helen had not met, she saw their circle grow and change. It was a healthy thing, she thought.

Three hours flew by, during which time they ordered various hors d'oeuvres and called it dinner. At 9:00 p.m., the group began to disperse. She offered Ryan and Lilly a ride home, but they were going to catch an Uber so she could head straight home herself. She appreciated that; she wanted to get home to her bed. And she hoped she was physically fatigued to the point where her mind would not keep her up all night, worrying about Marty and saving the world. She silently hoped she would not have to choose between the two.

CHAPTER 26

Emma had been called to in-person auditions for several of the parts she and Angela had sent files to. Next week would be the first callback, and it was at Steppenwolf Theatre on Halsted, the North Side of the city.

Angela regretted that she couldn't go with Emma to the auditions. She was so invested in the process that she felt part of it, and she'd have liked to be there to support Emma. However, she knew she was not safe wandering around in public at this point.

Frances had told her about Rooney's endeavors on the illegal side of life, and she was disgusted at her own involvement with him. She asked Frances what she thought about her doing counseling online in order to explore how she'd become embroiled with his life. Since she had been at the house, she'd begun to bring in a healthy income, so it wasn't a question of paying for it. Frances, of course, supported the idea.

Angela had also started to do some investigative work for Frances's friend Parker's firm. Parker had been very complimentary about her skills when they worked together to create a secure IP address for her business. Maybe they were giving Rooney too much credit to think he could find her online, but he had enough money to pay someone else to do it, so it was better to be safe than sorry.

That work, as well as her work with Emma, and the freelance coding she was doing in response to RFPs on the web kept her busy and happy. Life was interesting, although she missed her time with her sisters and friends from the neighborhood. She had managed, through Parker, to get a message to one of her sisters to let her know she was in a safe place away from Rooney and that she should not share with him or anyone else that they'd heard from her.

"Eventually, dear, you'll be able to safely move about again," Frances had assured her. "Just give Parker a little time to keep tabs on Mr. Hardy. When he says it's safe, you'll know it is safe indeed."

She trusted Frances. Period.

CHAPTER 27

Johnathan Richards sat on the terrace overlooking the ocean at Malibu. His girlfriend, Marta, emerged through the sliding doors in a string bikini and a sheer cover-up, adding to the beauty of the scene. She handed him the perfect cocktail and sat down.

"I'll be heading out of town tomorrow for two days of meetings. When I get back, I'll need to stay in LA to be closer to the office," he said.

"I have a photo shoot in Hawaii next week," Marta shared. "We can meet back here to celebrate Valentine's Day together?" she asked.

"Absolutely," Johnathan replied. "There will be a lot to celebrate this year."

CHAPTER 28

Parker was looking forward to his team meeting this morning. He had several pieces of information about the Chicago situation and assumed others would too. The challenge at this point would be to see if they connected in any way.

Once they'd all joined the Zoom call, Parker began by saying he'd like to hear from them about a variety of cases. They moved through the agenda, ending with the discussion of the Chicago gang movements.

"What do you have, Patty? You're on the ground in the Midwest," said Parker.

"We believe there must be something coming into the city on the fourteenth. There are no current turf battles among the gangs right now; in fact, they seem to be cooperating better than they normally do. That alone is a clue. There is an individual who has been serving as a broker between the gangs when big opportunities present themselves, and we've been observing his comings and goings now for a while. I don't know that he's involved in whatever this is, but he's certainly a nexus point for gang stuff, so we'll keep an eye on him with this situation in mind and see if we find any connection. His name is Joey Caruso. He seems to have made some lucrative connections by providing drugs to the movie company employees who've been working on productions in Chicago. They bring a lot of people into town with them from the West Coast, and some of those people have habits that need servicing, which would suggest to me a possible trail in that direction. What do you think, Lorraine?" Patty asked.

Lorraine Evangelista was the West Coast region's leader. She agreed there could be a connection and would be looking for travel between the coast and Chicago by the dealmakers they were aware of. The problem was the dealmakers they weren't aware of. "But we'll keep an eye out, and please keep us informed if Joey is receiving guests from this region."

"Great. Guy? Byron?" Parker asked his leaders from the southern and northern regions if they had anything yet. Neither did.

"I'd like to change our focus then," Parker said. "Frances has a resident at her house—not Angela, who we've worked with a bit—but a young man named Marty. Marty was a gang member in Chicago before being sentenced for drug trafficking. He was also a user but has been clean and is on the straight and narrow now. Trouble is his gang is still approaching him when he goes into the city to do his bloodwork, trying to find out if he's coming back as soon as his supervision ends, which is next month."

He continued, "When they approached him earlier this week, they alluded to something big going down and told him his experience would be of great value to them and that he'd be well compensated for his efforts.

"Marty told them he'd think about it in order to bring them along. He has since offered to gain their trust in order to find out more about the activity," Parker concluded.

"Brave kid," Patty said.

"Risky," Byron added.

"Right on both counts," Parker said. "Frances has asked his caseworker, Helen, if she would support this. She, like Frances, fears for the kid's safety. Frances said she will only encourage him in this if we can monitor the whole interaction and step in if any threat arises.

"My question," he concluded, "is can we confidently do that? And who would like to work with me to choreograph this meeting?"

Four voices said, "I will," at the same time.

● ⸵ ⸱ ⁕

Helen and Frances had begun talking each day at around 3:00 p.m., and each day Donald answered and would end up wearing an apron. It was the one cheerful moment of each call, after which things became much more serious.

"Well, it is a pleasure to talk with you as usual, dear. Thank you for calling," Frances said. "I do have some news today. I spoke with my PI connection, and he is working up a plan to monitor Marty's interaction with his former gang members around his next blood test at Stroger. He will review that plan with Marty to see if it is in line with the way the gang would go about things. So that's in the works."

"And I've talked with my boss, Tom, and he's talked to the city detectives," Helen said. "They, of course, are not thrilled about being sidelined. They prefer to be the point on anything like this. Tom was firm with them though, saying that if they want help from our clients, they will have to work our way. This is a new thing for them and for us. I'm not sure we'd get away with this again, but this time they have reluctantly conceded."

"Great. And we're having to move quickly on these things. It's the end of January. We only have a couple weeks," Frances said. "I have no idea how two nice girls like ourselves have become embroiled in this nasty business, but I guess it's too late to back out now.

"I appreciate you, Helen," Frances concluded.

"And I appreciate you, Frances," Helen replied.

CHAPTER 29

Helen had been meeting with Maggie weekly and talking with her every few days since she started her part-time job and moved into the rooming house Helen had found for her. Maggie seemed to be trying, Helen thought. She was showing up at work and sounded engaged by what was going on.

Of course, Maggie being Maggie, there was always some entertaining commentary on her coworkers and the patrons who came through the burger and chicken place where she worked.

She seemed to be interested in any progress on the matter she had reported to the city detectives. And she mentioned it from time to time to Helen.

As Helen got ready to run down to grab lunch one day, her cell phone rang. The caller ID showed the store where Maggie was working. She hoped Maggie was behaving.

"This is Helen," she answered.

"Helen, it's Maggie. I asked to use the phone here for a quick call to you. They think it's something I'm required to do for my probation, so play along if they bring it up, OK?

Anyway, I just had some gang guys come through the drive-through, and they recognized me. In fact, they like my new hairstyle, but I digress. They invited me to one of their little soirees tonight. I am having dinner with the Prince of Wales; otherwise I would, of course, attend. The location is the bar off the alley just south of Fullerton, between the Kennedy Expressway and Logan, called Bernie's. Just thought the cops might like to know. And you can tell them that I will only continue to help them do their jobs for so long without compensation."

"Thank you, Maggie. You are a princess, which is why, I assume, you would be dining with the Prince of Wales," Helen replied.

"Exactly," Maggie said.

On her way out, she left a note on Tom's desk with the information provided by Maggie.

CHAPTER 30

Johnathan Richards had a pleasant business class flight from LA to Chicago, arriving around dinnertime. He was picked up by his regular driver and chauffeured to the club, where he freshened up and had a lovely dinner with a perfectly paired wine.

He would meet with his investors tomorrow evening but wanted to get Joey's report before he saw them, to ensure that things were progressing without problems.

He took an Uber to LeBar on Chestnut, where Joey was already seated in a booth.

"Hey, Johnny, how ya doin'?" he said in some foreign language that Johnathan had to relearn every time he landed in Chicago.

"Great, Joe," Johnathan replied. "How are things going?"

"Good," Joey replied. "In fact, really good. Everything's in place on our end, and we're assumin' you have the logistics for delivery and offloading of product in place."

At this point, a young man came to the table to take their drink order.

"Dirty martini, please," Johnathan said.

"Dirty beer, please," Joey joked. "No, seriously, bring me a Budweiser, in a bottle."

"Everything is in place and will be delivered to the rail yard at the appointed time," Johnathan said, a bit condescendingly. What did these people think? This was some sort of amateur hour?

At this point, Johnathan regretted having ordered a drink. He was ready for this meeting to be over. What would he and Joey talk about for the next half hour?

He barely survived with the help of one of the best dirty martinis he'd ever tasted, after which he Ubered back to the club. Tomorrow evening, he'd report to his investors, and at next quarter's meeting, they'd be expecting a new investment plan from him.

CHAPTER 31

It was a typical morning at the house. Residents were up and about, following the scent of coffee like blind mice smelling cheese. The dining room was quiet except for the sounds of chairs being pulled out, coffee being poured, and occasional yawning. Freezing rain was pelting the windows, and the unspoken consensus was that all humanity should head back to bed with a book.

After choosing either a scone or English muffin, the residents plodded toward their respective areas of the house to work, with very little verbal communication breaking the silence.

Even Marty seemed to be plinking away on the piano rather than creating beautiful runs of random melodies that typically ran through his head and out his fingers the first time he sat down at the piano in the morning.

The silence was broken by the ringing of the phone from the office. Donald picked it up as he was in motion between the dining room and the library.

"Good morning?" he answered skeptically.

"And good morning to you, Mr. Fernandez!" a way too cheerful voice answered.

"Ah, what a pleasant intonation you have, Mr. Bennett," Donald answered. "What is it that makes you so cheerful on a miserable day like this one?"

"Well, I have talked with my team," Parker continued, "and I believe we have an excellent plan for keeping your young resident safe during his next visit to Chicago. I'd like to run it by him to see if it seems like it flows with what his gang contacts would find normal."

"That is excellent news!" Donald replied, a bit more chipper this time. "I'll get him for you. And, Parker, thank you. We are so grateful to you."

"Say nothing of it, Don. It is my pleasure. I am very happy to help."

Donald went to the parlor. "Marty, the call is for you. It's Parker Bennett. He'd like to run something by you."

Marty moved from the parlor to the office and closed the doors. "Hello, Mr. Bennett. It's Marty."

"Hi, Marty! From the tone of Mr. Fernandez's voice, it sounds like you all may be getting a slow start today."

Marty laughed. "Yep. Like molasses."

"I wanted to run our ideas by you, Marty, to see if they'd ring true with what your gang colleagues would expect. If not, at any point, please stop me."

"Yes, thank you. I will," Marty replied.

Parker then described the scenario he and his team had come up with. Marty listened intently and with very few alterations, affirming that the whole plan flowed very well.

"I will share the plan with Frances and Donald if that is

acceptable to you, Marty," Parker concluded. "They are very concerned for your safety, as I'm sure you know."

At this point, there was a pause in the conversation. Parker knew Marty was attempting to compose himself.

"Excuse me, Mr. Bennett, I'm not used to having people around me who care for me the way Frances, Donald, and the rest of my roommates do. It is a wonderful thing. I hope I do them proud."

"And my team and I will be there to help you, Marty."

The call ended. Marty got up from the chair by the phone to head back to the parlor, where Zachary was probably dozing in a chair. The phone began to ring again. Such a strange sound so early in the morning—or at all.

"Um, hello?" Marty said tentatively.

"Hello, mate, I'm wondering if I may speak to Mr. Zachary Birmingham or his colleague Marty Munos?" the caller said.

If Marty wasn't mistaken, this person had an English accent.

"Yes, this is Marty Munos."

"Excellent. This is Bernie Taupin. I was talking with Bono last evening at a charity event, and your names came up. I've listened to your stuff online, and it is amazing. Elton and I are working with well-known artists in the music business to feature songs by up-and-coming songwriters like yourselves—kind of passing the baton, if you will. We'll be making an album of the songs, recorded by those established artists. We'd like to talk with you about using some of your songs and, eventually, to sit down with you for a session to see what we can create together—Elton with you, composing music, Zachary with me on lyrics."

"One moment, please," Marty said. "I'd like to get Zachary."

And at the risk of disturbing the peace, Marty quietly laid down the phone, walked to the hallway, shut the heavy, wooden pocket doors, and yelled at the top of his lungs, "Zachary, Bernie Taupin and Elton John want to work with us!"

Thunderous footsteps were heard from all corners of the house as the residents stampeded toward the office. They were now fully awake and wanted to hear this call.

CHAPTER 32

The following evening, Johnathan was chauffeured to Kenilworth for a meeting with the investors. Ida greeted him at the door. Max and his colleagues were in the parlor enjoying cocktails before dinner. They were all excited to see Johnathan.

The dinner conversation was cheerful and positive. Johnathan had confirmed that they could each expect a $1 million return on their $100,000 investment, as per their last joint venture. What Johnathan didn't mention was that he'd be making $5 million on their investment. But they were happy with their return; who wouldn't be? Besides, he was taking all the risk, or most of it anyway.

After dinner, they toasted their collaboration and headed home. Johnathan's chauffeured ride brought him to the door of the Lake Shore Club without a word. And everything was set to move forward without a hitch.

What Johnathan hadn't noticed, however, was that one of Parker's guys had been at LeBar the previous evening, tailing Joey. They photo ID'd Johnathan Richards and researched his background, finding that Johnathan had been a neighborhood thug in West LA as a youth, involved with gangs and arrested several times, serving in juvenile detention. Of course, his name, at that time, had been Owen Brown. As good fortune would have it, Owen's good looks began to show through in a town where good looks are a ticket to success. He polished up his grammar and language by working as a doorman at the Hollywood Hilton, where he was discovered by some wealthy but lonely society ladies. Eventually, he was able to quit the front door and move inside the hotel, where he continued to serve special clients.

As it happened, Johnathan learned a lot about business around these people and realized he was very good with numbers. He brokered a few small deals for them, saying he had connections, which he did. They didn't exactly understand what kind of connections he had, but they were aware that the returns they got from doing deals with Johnathan were quite high.

Through those connections, he met Max and his Kenilworth investors.

Parker's guys knew who Johnathan was now and what type of investments he brokered. He had a fairly broad range of *products*, but the common thread was their distribution, which was always through urban gangs.

They followed him to Max's house that night and watched from a distance by high-powered lens as the blue-blood investors exited Max's house. They ID'd them too.

Now they had the link to the gangs. It was just a matter of figuring out what they were up to.

CHAPTER 33

Frances drove Marty and Zachary to the train at 6:00 a.m., just as she had done the previous month. She told them she loved them both as they exited the car and that she'd be waiting to retrieve them when they came back later today.

Once in the city, they jumped on the El, exiting at the Stroger stop. It was a short walk to the clinic from there. Marty checked in. Zachary went for coffee and doughnuts. Marty was surprised to see Paolo sitting across the waiting room with Sammy, the leader of their gang. They motioned for him to join them as soon as Zachary walked out of the waiting area. Marty wasn't sure who it was in the waiting room, but he knew Parker also had someone watching. He moved over to sit between them.

"Hey, Mart," Sammy said. "You're looking great. Incarceration must agree with you."

"Hey, Sam," Marty replied, "good to see you," and they bumped fists all around.

"Paolo told me about your chat last month. This is your last check-in then? And after this, your supervision is over?" Sammy confirmed.

"Right," Marty said.

"Great. Well, listen. We'd love to see you get back with the guys where you belong. We need the manpower, and everyone knows you're good at what you do—and smart. What's your plan?" Sammy asked.

"Oh, no plan really. Just staying in a temporary community place right now. But that ends, as you know, when the supervision is over," Marty said.

"We'd like you to come to town to meet with us soon. Is there a way you can make a loop through town? We have some business to discuss," Sammy concluded.

"Sure," Marty replied. "I'll be back later this week. Can we meet at the coffee place across the street, say Wednesday morning at ten?"

"Sounds good," Sammy replied. "Gotta go." Paolo and Sammy got up and exited the room. Zachary, who had been waiting and watching from the corridor, walked up to Marty with coffee and doughnuts from the cafeteria and sat down next to him, just as they called Marty's name for bloodwork.

When the test was over, they headed back to the train, Marty ate his doughnut, and they sat in silence.

When Marty and Zachary got back to the house, they ate with the others. Frances told them Parker wanted to debrief Marty after lunch. Frances got Parker on the phone in the office and left the room.

"Hey, Marty," Parker said. "Everything go OK?"

"Yes, thank you," Marty replied.

"Want to share?"

"Sure," Marty said, and he reviewed what had gone on when he met with Sammy and Paolo.

"OK then, you'll be meeting with them at the coffee shop across from the Stroger Clinic entrance on Wednesday morning at ten. We'll be there. My team will meet and choreograph the various moves the gang guys could make and how we'll keep you safe in different scenarios. We'll do that this afternoon, and you and I can talk again tomorrow. You can react to the plan, like we did last time, and fine-tune it," Parker said.

"That sounds good, Mr. Bennett. And thank you again," Marty said.

"Listen, Marty, just to be clear, you have options. You don't have to put yourself in this situation," Parker said. "You've had your last blood test and can simply not show up on Wednesday. They won't find you, and you'll be safe."

"I know. I am making a choice. Thank you again, Mr. Bennett," Marty said. The call was over.

•⋮·•

The next day, Parker Bennett met online with his regional leaders. He explained that the gang leader had shown up to talk with Marty this time, again expressing their desire for him to get on board quickly because of an imminent deal requiring skilled laborers. Marty had agreed to meet with them at a coffee shop across the street from the hospital on Wednesday, which was tomorrow.

"We need a plan to ensure that the gang doesn't simply take Marty—that is, escort him to a car and drive away with him," Parker said. "The objective of the meeting is for Marty to learn everything he can about the event they're recruiting him for. Somehow Marty will need to gain their trust and then get away from them and back to the house for safety. Once he's safe, we can go over it all with him. I'm sure he'll have insights into unspoken things that will help us get a bigger picture.

"Realistically," Parker continued, "Marty should wear a wire. That way, should anything happen to him, we would have the conversation and be able to analyze it. As we all know, the wire would put Marty at greater risk."

Byron Slattery, northern regional leader of Parker's PI organization, BenMil, Ltd., had been outside Stroger watching what type of coverage the gang members had when they met with Marty in the waiting room.

"I haven't been able to figure out why Marty is so important to the gang leadership," Byron said, commenting on the fact that Sammy himself had wanted to meet with him. "Could it really be just because they are badly in need of rank-and-file soldiers at this point? Or is there some other reason?"

Parker said, "I wondered the same thing, Byron."

Patty Daley, central region leader, said, "Well, I watched them meet from across the waiting room." She had been outfitted with a large belly to look pregnant. "I wondered the same thing. But it is clear they want him. I don't know how intently they track and re-recruit others from the gang who've done time, but this seems excessive to me."

"He could have intersected some of their contacts in prison. Sometimes unwitting messengers are created through informal conversation. If someone had a conversation with Marty in prison, and the gang leadership debriefed him, seemingly casually, a message or signal could be passed," Guy Padilla of the southern region commented.

"Or he could be the stooge they intend to pin everything on if this deal starts to fall apart," Parker said. "We've seen that before too."

"All I know is this Owen Brown, a.k.a., Johnathan Richards, is a bad dude," said Lorraine Evangelista, leader from the west. "I don't know what they're up to, but I know that if it's being orchestrated by Brown/Richards, it involves a lot of money and a lot of gangs and will harm many people."

"OK, then," Parker said. "How are we going to keep this kid safe? And I want you to know that I offered him an out. He refused. He's a brave kid. He knows what happens to people who cross these guys, but he still wants to go forward. He really is a great kid at heart, according to Frances and Donald. We need to ensure he walks back from this meeting and returns safely home to them."

Marty talked with Parker after his meeting with the regional leaders of BenMil. Parker described where pickets would be posted around the coffee shop when Marty met Sammy. He asked Marty if there were ways he'd seen the gang abduct people.

Marty said, "Yes. I've watched them take people out back doors of buildings, take them into elevators, exiting midway up a tall building and locking the elevator while heading up or down in the stairwell. I've seen them cause disturbances in restaurants, or just outside the front window, exiting the building in the chaos they caused. I've seen them draw a big crowd onto the street and make their way with the person they were abducting through that crowd, and I've seen cars pull up, grab the person, and speed away. There are as many ways as you can think of."

"OK," Palmer said. "We'll have someone in both the men's and women's restrooms. We'll have someone on the street in front and the alley in back. The cashier will be one of our staff members. I think we've covered all your scenarios but the elevator one. Unfortunately, the coffee shop is in front of a large office building, so there's room for them to maneuver. We'll have someone by the elevators."

"Does that sound OK to you?" Parker asked.

"Yes, sir," Marty responded.

"And what about the wire?" Parker asked.

"I think it makes sense, Mr. Bennett. Particularly if they don't find it on me!" Marty replied, indicating that he understood the consequences if they did.

"Well, the technology is very sophisticated these days. The mic and earphone are really micro. You could practice dropping it if they somehow got close enough to find it. Hell, you could even swallow the thing it's so small. It will be in your mail today when Frances picks it up. Take a look at it."

"I will practice, Mr. Bennett." Marty replied. "And thank you."

"No, Marty. Thank you," Parker replied.

CHAPTER 34

Helen's desk phone rang around four thirty. It was Maggie Dax, calling from work again; at least she always hoped it was Maggie and not the owner talking about Maggie causing problems or not showing up to work.

"This is Helen," she said.

"Hey, what's up, buttercup?" Maggie asked.

"Well, hello there, Miss Mag. How's work today?" Helen replied.

"Great, as usual" was Maggie's sarcastic reply.

"Did you tell them you needed to check in with me as part of your probation again?" Helen asked.

"I did," Maggie said proudly. "They don't want to impede my rehabilitation, so they never give me a hard time. Especially since they are all as dumb as a box o' rocks, and I'll probably be their boss soon. How hard can it be to make a sandwich, Helen? Tell me."

"It depends on the sandwich, Maggie ... always depends on the sandwich," Helen replied.

"Oh, Helen," Maggie responded. "We gotta toughen

you up. You are just too generous in your interpretations of what goes on around you."

"Thank you, Maggie. I'll look forward to that toughening. Gotta go now though, unless you have intel to pass along."

"I actually do have some intel, Helen! I almost forgot! I got invited to another party, and I think I'm going this time. It's tonight at nine in Humboldt Park. Just thought I'd blow through there to see what I could hear. Get that? I'm going to *see* what I can *hear*."

Concerned, Helen answered, "Are you sure that's a good idea, Maggie? You could get stuck in the middle of something bad with that crowd."

"Helen," Maggie said, "I've been stuck in the middle of something bad since I was born; you just weren't around to be worried. Now you are. That's all that's changed. Besides, I'm getting good at this Sherlock Holmes thing, and I don't want to lose my edge due to lack of practice."

"You better call me when you get in tonight, or early tomorrow morning. I'm going to be up all night," Helen replied.

"No phone, Helen. Remember?"

I gotta figure out how to get her a phone. Even a burner would ease my mind. Helen wrote herself a note.

"Right. Great. Ugh. OK, Maggie. I'm serious. Be careful, or I'm gonna get a dog to guard you twenty-four seven. You scare the crap outta me," Helen said.

"I'll be fine," Maggie replied. Helen was not reassured.

Helen went home, ate something, and began to worry about Maggie. She couldn't help it. She felt responsible for her because she knew Maggie planned to go to the party, and Helen hadn't tried hard enough to stop her. But what could she have done? She had told Tom on her way to the elevator that there was a gang gathering in the Humboldt Park neighborhood at nine o'clock tonight and that Maggie would be there doing reconnaissance, so if he could let his law enforcement friends know not to arrest Maggie, it would be helpful.

"Do you know how many gang parties will be going on at that same time in that same neighborhood, Helen?" he replied.

"No," Helen replied. "Please don't tell me," she said as she walked away from his office doorway.

Around 8:30 p.m., Helen noticed a text from Lilly. "Hi, Lennie. Got any time tomorrow to meet me somewhere downtown? I have something I need to discuss with you."

"Sure," Helen replied. "Just text me toward the end of the day, and we'll make a plan. Thanks."

CHAPTER 35

Frances dropped Marty at the train the next morning. Zachary was not with him this time. They weren't sure where the gang members would begin to observe him. Did they know he came in on this train? There was no telling without more time to observe them. And they didn't have time. This whole plan, whatever it was, was supposed to go down next week on Valentine's Day. They had to find out what it was and do something about it soon.

Marty transferred to the El and got off at the Stroger station. He walked briskly toward the clinic, turning into the café right across the street from it.

He looked around but didn't see anyone familiar, so he sat down in a booth. There were very few people in the restaurant between breakfast and lunch. A few here and there, but it was not full by any means.

The waitress came to the table. He ordered a Coke and fries. She walked off.

A huge noise came from the kitchen, where someone had apparently dropped a pan. He about jumped out of the booth. Everyone else turned to look toward the kitchen but then returned to their conversations or the food they were eating. No big deal.

It was 10:15. He had been in the restaurant for twenty-five minutes, eaten his fries, and had a refill on his Coke. The waitress asked if he wanted anything else. When he said no, she slid the check across the table to him and looked at him like he should seize the moment by moving out of her station and back onto the street. He was kind of nervous, so the look could have meant something else entirely, he thought.

At 10:25, he got up and went to the door. He looked both ways, up and down the street. He saw nothing. Looking around, he wasn't sure who Parker's employees were and who were patrons of the restaurant, so he shrugged and walked out the door, proceeding down the street to the El station. As he entered the station building to descend the stairs to the platform, two guys he did not know were coming off the platform and approaching the turnstile. They each grabbed an arm, dragged Marty backward to the street. They threw him into a car, and that car sped away.

Parker's guys were coming up behind Marty, observing the abduction firsthand. They touched their earbuds to transmit the information to the others.

"The car sped away to the south and then east. It was a gray, Chevy SUV. Shit!"

CHAPTER 36

Helen awoke with a start. It was 7:30 a.m., and she was out cold. She hadn't fallen asleep last night until about three, wondering what was going on with Maggie and knowing Marty would have his meeting with the gang guys in the morning.

She rushed around, showering, dressing, drying her hair, applying makeup, warming up Edith, which was no small feat these days, and beginning her commute.

When she got to work, she checked her messages. Nothing from Maggie. Marty would be on the train about now, heading down for his meeting.

This was going to be one of those days.

She cruised by Tom's office for a chat, since she wasn't doing too well focusing on anything. Tom had relayed information to the detectives about the party Maggie was going to. They promised to keep an eye out for her if they interacted with any of the partygoers. He hadn't heard anything from any of them, so "no news is good news," he told Helen.

At noon, Helen got up to walk down to Chipotle. She

needed to burn off some excess energy. As she walked past Tom's office, he was shouting into the phone. Very un-Tom-like. "You did what? I told you she'd be there. You know her. Everyone knows her. Why do you let her bait you? Get a grip on your officers, would you? We'll be right down to get her."

He turned around, looked at Helen, and said, "Go pick up Maggie, would you? She's being held at the Sixteenth Precinct police station."

"Is she OK?" Helen asked anxiously.

"She's fine, but I'm going to have a heart attack dealing with that young woman one of these days," he said.

She exited the building toward the parking garage rather than toward Chipotle.

As she passed Deluxe, a great burger place adjacent to the parking garage, she saw Lilly and Ryan having lunch. She went to knock on the window just as she saw Ryan lean toward Lilly, giving her a kiss on the cheek. They were holding hands.

Her first impulse was to disappear as quickly as possible. She was embarrassed to have witnessed this moment between her two best friends. Then she remembered she was supposed to meet Lilly later today, because Lilly had something to talk to her about.

She guessed she knew what that something was. She was shocked and hurt and humiliated and upset, but she didn't know why. This was what she had asked for, although she hadn't realized the next development would be for her best friend and her longtime boyfriend to quickly become a couple.

It would have to wait. She needed to get Maggie before she committed a felony or something in the lockup.

CHAPTER 37

Marty's head was pushed down between his knees in the back seat of an SUV. He had not recognized these guys. He didn't know whether to hope they were Sammy's guys or some other guys. He just waited to see what would happen next, and that might very well be a massive car accident the way this guy was driving down narrow side streets with parked cars on both sides.

They stopped a short distance from the hospital. He knew that because they were in the car a relatively short period of time. They pulled into a garage and told him to get out of the car. They took him to Sammy.

"Hey, bro," Sammy said.

"Geez, Sam, that was dramatic. I thought we were meeting for coffee," Marty said, acting a bit put out. He hoped he was acting cool and in character, but who knew what they were thinking? He sure didn't.

"Yeah, well, too public. This thing we have going down is big, Mart. Big money, lotsa moving parts. Not something to talk about in public places," Sammy said.

"OK. That's cool. What do you need from me?" Marty asked.

"Let's sit down. Paulie, get us each a beer," Sammy said to one of his staff, and off that person went. Sammy was clearly the don these days.

"Here's the deal, Marty," Sammy said, leaning forward over his beer and toward Marty, like they were buddies sharing a secret.

"We have a big shipment coming in next week. I need someone I can trust to receive that shipment at our warehouse and wire the payment to the vendor's account. That would need to be someone I could really trust, Mart. My question is, can I really trust you? I assume you're interested in getting back into the flow of things now that you're out and when you get off probation. Is that a correct assumption, Marty?"

"That's what I did last time, isn't it, Sammy?" Marty answered.

"It is," Sammy said. "I just have some big stuff going on, and the timing sucks. Typically, I'd work you back in slowly to find out where your head's at, Marty. I just don't have the time to do that this time. All I can say is that if you are willing to make this commitment now, and you pull it off without a glitch, you will be set for a long time. The money is big on this Marty, and about $100,000 of it would be yours."

"Whew," said Marty and gave out a little whistle. "That would be great if I could go from a jail cell to a condo. What's the next step?"

"Well, first of all, let's have a little welcome-home party, shall we?" Sammy said. Two guys walked toward the table and, moving to either side of Marty, grabbing him under the arms, held him tightly. Sammy approached Marty with a syringe. He tapped it to get the bubbles out and injected the liquid substance into Marty's arm.

"There. You should feel pretty good right about now, Mart. This one's on the house. I just wanted to know you'd get back here as soon as possible. There's more where this came from, but you can only get it this pure here, so I hope you won't take too much time to get whatever it is you need from wherever it's been you're staying and get back here."

Sammy told the two guys to take him back to the El platform where they'd picked him up and let him out. He turned to Marty and said, "I'll expect you back here by midnight tonight. The guys will pick you up at the Stroger station. Welcome back, Marty."

CHAPTER 38

Helen parked and entered the Sixteenth Precinct.

"Here for Maggie, I presume?" the officer at the desk said to her.

"I am," Helen answered. "But how did you know?"

"Oh, she described you. She said it would be like Pollyanna and Mother Teresa's child had gone into social work," he said and chuckled.

"Great," Helen said, blushing. "Just great."

She was taken back to a small room where she signed the discharge papers. Maggie came in with an elated look on her face. She put her finger to her lips as though she had a secret she didn't want to share in this place.

As they emerged from the building, Maggie could barely contain herself. Helen couldn't understand why she was so excited. She'd just been arrested—again. When would the girl have enough?

"Helen," Maggie gushed, "it wasn't easy to get arrested last night, but I needed to stay with the woman I was hanging with at the party. Her boyfriend is a big-time gangbanger, and she was going on and on about the fancy car he was gonna buy her next week, and the diamond ring he was gonna buy her next week, and the lakefront condo he was gonna move her into next week. As she drank more and more, and smoked more and more weed, I began to ask her about the money. Where was it coming from?"

"You are incorrigible Maggie!" Helen interrupted. "I told them you'd be at the party and not to arrest you."

"Yep. I could tell. That's why I had to get really obnoxious. They were determined not to take me in, no matter what."

"What did you do to them, Maggie?" Helen asked. "I mean to get them to arrest you."

Maggie said, "I'll get to that. But I gotta finish the first part. This gal, Tiffanie, was just about to give me a few details, and in comes Barney Fife and the Keystone Cops. I couldn't stop at that point. I'd been working hard to get to this point all night, and here they come."

Helen rolled her eyes. Just like Marcia Brady.

Maggie continued, "I needed to get it out of her on the ride to the station, because once they gave her coffee and started asking questions to book her, she'd sober up. I asked where the money was coming from.

"She said, 'A big deal.'

"I said, 'That must be a really big deal if he's gonna make that much.'

"She said, 'Oh, it is. All the gangs across the city are in on it. That'll just be his individual portion. There are lots of guys involved.'

"I asked, 'What's the product?'

"She said, 'Guns, I think. He's gonna get a few new ones. He's excited.'

"I asked, 'Where are they coming from?'"

"She said, 'On a train from somewhere out of the country. It's international business. He's a very important businessman.'"

"And then she fell asleep on my shoulder, which was disgusting, but we were almost to the station, and I was grateful to her for getting so fucked up she didn't know what she was telling me and wouldn't remember any of it in the morning," Maggie concluded.

"Very cool, eh, Punky Brewster?" Maggie concluded.

"Yes. Very cool. And call me Mother Teresa," Helen replied. "Oh, and I'm still curious about what you did to get yourself arrested."

"Well, it wasn't one thing," Maggie said with a grin. "It was more like a series of things. First, I dropped to all fours and tried to bite one cop on the leg. He shook me off though. I then grabbed the Tiffanie chick and began screaming that she was a zombie. I took off my shoe and threw it at another cop. And then I began to swear like a sailor while doing somersaults, and I was wearing a skirt and no underwear. I feel like they took me to the station for my own safety, but that was fine. I just needed to go to the station with Tiffanie."

"Very creative," Helen said as she rolled her eyes, once again. "So proud."

She took Maggie back to her rooming house to get cleaned up and then took her to the office. Tom called the city detectives to come over and hear what Maggie had to say.

It was at this point that Helen was called out of the meeting. There was an urgent phone call, she was told.

CHAPTER 39

It was Frances, who was distraught. Marty had been abducted. His wire had relayed all he'd learned from his gang contacts, but he'd been injected with heroin. He was expected back at the gang headquarters at midnight tonight, ready for another injection and to settle in with the rest of the gang in preparation for next week.

Helen was horrified. "I am so sorry, Frances!"

Frances said, "As am I, dear. Parker is distraught. He is appalled they were unable to protect Marty from this. The real question now is where we go from here. If Marty doesn't go back, they'll know he's out in the environment with information. If he goes into rehab, they'll know exactly where to find him because all services are provided to him at Stroger. I assume he'd be at Stroger because he's under supervision until the end of the month. Is that right, dear?

"That's correct, Frances," Helen interjected.

"If he does go back, they'll continue to inject him with heroin, to keep him under their control. It's a horror story," Frances concluded.

"Thank you for telling me, Frances, although I wish

it weren't true. I need to check in with Parker about some information Maggie got last night, so I'll talk to him next. I hope he has an amazing solution that will fix everything," Helen concluded, realizing this was a Pollyanna thought.

Helen headed back to the meeting with Tom and the city detectives and told them about the call with Frances. She saw Maggie perk up; she was all ears.

It was time for the city and Parker's people and the FBI to get together. It was now clear that this thing was international, national, and local in scope.

When Helen looked at her phone. It was almost 4:00 p.m. She checked for messages, and there was a text from Lilly asking her to meet at Fortissimo, a little piano bar in the Loop.

"I apologize, Lill, but all hell's breaking loose here, and I don't think I'll get out until 10:00 tonight. Can I take a raincheck until the weekend?" she texted.

"Sure. I guess. I was really hoping to get together. Don't work yourself to death," Lilly responded.

Marty was dropped on the Stroger El platform by the guys who'd taken him from there in the first place. He was in a fog but made his way to the train and back to the parking lot. Parker and his team knew of the situation due to Marty's wire and had notified Frances that he was on his way back. She was waiting.

They had not gone into detail with Frances about what they'd overheard. Marty explained it to them all when they got back to the house.

"I'm already back on the heroin," he said, "and we know enough about what's going down that Parker's guys should be able to find me when the illegal stuff is distributed. They know I'll be doing money at the North Side location, unless Sammy lied about that.

"Either way, I'd like to see this through," he finished. "At this point, it's too late to play it safe. If I wear the wire and the information continues to flow, it could make a huge difference in how this thing goes down. I want to help."

It was hard for Frances, Parker, Donald, and the others to appreciate that Marty was comfortable with this environment to some extent. Not that he was at ease in it, but it was not unfamiliar to him. And ultimately, they couldn't stop him, other than putting him back in jail. It was his choice, and it was very courageous, because they all knew it could save many, many lives.

The goodbyes that night were sad and sorrowful. Frances and Donald drove Marty to the train. He took it to the El and then took the El to the Stroger Hospital platform. At midnight, the guys who had collected him earlier that day pulled up, and he got into the car.

He was dropped off at a garage on the North Side, where he was injected with more heroin. He was directed to a cot, where he passed into oblivion.

When Marty awoke the next day, he realized there were several other guys in the room on cots. The other guys kept their distance from him, either because they figured he was a junkie, who was so important he was being supplied by Sammy, or he was fucked. They didn't want to get in the way of whatever Sammy was doing with this guy.

After several days and nights of this, Marty wasn't thinking particularly clearly, something for which he was grateful. He understood that he was back in the middle of this hell he had been bound and determined not to get back into. He also knew he was helping. For whatever it was worth, he'd worn a wire, and they heard what he heard. Hopefully they'd be able to piece it all together, and some good would come from it.

What he did know was that tonight was the night it would all go down, and then he would leave. If they shot him in the back on his way out or staged some kind of accident when all the deals were done and they didn't need him anymore, it didn't matter to him. Death would be preferable to another cycle of addiction, arrest, court, jail, probation, gang stalking, again and again. He'd had enough. Better to go out having done something he was proud of than to go out a gangbanger junkie who'd never done a constructive thing in his life.

CHAPTER 40

On the morning of February 14, Valentine's Day, Helen got out of bed. It was the first time in four years she would have no card, no flowers, and no date, but none of that crossed her mind. She was up and out early, headed to work. Good thing Edith knew the way, because Helen didn't remember anything about the drive downtown on this day.

At the house, there were pastries from yesterday. The coffee was fresh, and there was an empty chair at the table. Very little was said, and very little had been said for the past week. That empty chair silently screamed and overcame any conversation that might have taken place normally.

Parker and his team were together, ready to implement a plan they'd coordinated with detectives from the city, as well as the FBI, to get Marty back safely. This was an interstate and international situation. Everyone who knew how to help needed to help.

And that included Maggie. Maggie was hanging out with Joey Caruso of all people. It turned out LeBar, where Joey and Johnathan had met, observed by Parker's team, was Joey's favorite watering hole in the city. The law enforcement guys and Parker's guys realized they had details about the North Side gangs but nothing about the West and South Side. Tired of Maggie's pleading, Parker and the detectives had reluctantly agreed to her involvement, but only at LeBar, where she could be watched.

Maggie started hanging around the bar every evening at the same time Joey typically came in. She, too, wore a wire. Helen had taken Maggie shopping, again, had her makeup done, and got her a mani-pedi. She made sure she was noticed the first night she entered LeBar. It didn't take long for Joey to notice her. He checked her out and found out from his guys that she was one of them, so to speak.

It had been a long time since Joey had talked to an intelligent woman who was also beautiful and a good listener. In the short few days since their first encounter, he'd regaled her with stories that demonstrated again and again his dominance over the dim-witted law enforcement officers.

"He is truly amazing," Maggie reported. "Just ask him."

That morning, there would be an online meeting between Parker's team, the city's team, Maggie, Tom and Helen, and Frances and Donald.

They had a lot to go over to prepare for the evening's events.

The meeting began at 8:00 a.m. Beverly Wainwright, the FBI lead in Chicago, chaired. Everyone introduced themselves. The agenda was put forth with a request for additional items for consideration.

Beverly began by expressing gratitude to Parker's team and to the caseworkers and their clients who had provided so much intel on this case. She continued, "We need to review what we're trying to accomplish today, and it's a lot. I'd ask everyone to be concise with your comments and stick to the agenda. We all have a lot going on and need to get back to it.

"The FBI will take care of the rooftop activity on North Sheridan. It will be timed to keep everyone safe but not to give the gangs too much notice that we're on to them. We are unsure how they will react to this intervention, since it is presumed this disturbance is their cover for the shipment. We will have to react to whatever contingency plan they may have in real time.

"In addition," Beverly continued, "the FBI agents, Chicago detectives, and Parker's team will all have people at the train yard. Parker's team will be involved with this since their goal is to retrieve Marty Munos, and we believe he will be at the north drop-off point.

"We know certain things, such as the timing, which we believe will coincide with the rooftop activity up north, specifically the dinner hour on Valentine's Day. What we don't know is which train or train car has the cargo. It could be one that's been standing in the yard for several days, or a stacked boxcar in storage, or one that's coming into the yard from somewhere else. We have transport documents on all the above, but we know they will have been falsified, so we'll be more dependent on observing the activity in the yard than on documents filed with the Department of Transportation. In other words, we won't know what's what until we begin to see trucks pulling up around a specific boxcar. And then we can't be seen, since we will need to stake out those trucks and follow them to their drop-off points in order to intersect all criminal personnel engaged in this activity. Parker's team has been tailing Joey Caruso, with Maggie Dax's assistance of course, this past week. We're not sure where he will be during all of this, but we have some ideas. He is to be brought into custody by the FBI," Beverly reported.

"Johnathan Richards is to be brought into custody by the FBI in Los Angeles," she continued, "and I'd like to give a special shout-out to Lorraine Evangelista on Parker's West Coast team for her excellent work related to this guy. He's the kingpin, so to speak. If we get him and take him out of action, we will make significant headway against gang activity in Chicago and other cities.

"And finally," she concluded, "Max Menninger and his colleagues are to be taken into custody and questioned by the FBI. We assume they'll have the best attorneys on earth to keep them out of jail and defend that they 'knew nothing about the product being bought and delivered,' but that's for the courts to deal with. All we can do is bring them in and cut off the financing for these illegal deals.

"And, Parker, perhaps you'd like to take this last one?" she said.

"Marty Munos must be retrieved safely and transported to Northwestern Hospital downtown for treatment for heroin addiction. He will be in a secure ward. They will be waiting for him. BenMil associates will coordinate this action. This will be our sole focus moving forward."

Parker concluded, "I do want to say we have found our collaboration with your office to be less painful than we had anticipated, Beverly. Thank you for working with us and trusting us. I understand that we're outsiders, but we had a real stake in this one because of Marty. He is a truly remarkable young man, and many lives will be saved, including his, if we all do our jobs tonight."

"Thank you, Parker. We've had a good experience as well," Beverly replied.

"Are there questions," she continued, "or information you believe has not been shared across teams but will be required to make decisions on the ground? If so, please share now." She paused. "If not, let's get to it. We have work to do."

Frances asked for a moment of silence, just as she always did prior to a meal. And with that, the call ended.

"And now we wait," Frances said to her housemates.

⁕⁑⁕

Parker had team members staked at the train yard.

Maggie went to LeBar, just in case Joey stopped in prior to going wherever he'd be while the whole plan went into motion. If he did show up, she, wearing her wire, would be able to let the team know he was heading out from there, and they'd follow him. The barback tonight was an FBI agent.

Helen was at work with Tom and his husband, Robert, who'd brought dinner. She had thought of going out to Frances's to be with the others but hoped she'd have a better chance of finding out what was happening by being closer to the action.

She also wanted to keep tabs on Maggie. She had asked her to get over to the office as soon as she was sure Joey either wasn't going to show up or as soon as Joey left LeBar, if he did show up. She wanted to know where Maggie was at all times tonight. She was concerned that Maggie might buy herself a Spiderman suit and try to single-handedly save the day.

CHAPTER 41

"I love this pizza," Tom said, kind of listlessly.

"Me too," Helen affirmed, trancelike.

"I feel like I'm gonna throw up from stress," Robert said.

"Thanks, Robert," Helen replied.

"What?" Robert asked.

"Didn't you say you liked my dress?" Helen asked.

"No. You're wearing jeans, Helen."

"Oh," Helen said.

Obviously, they were all distracted. And then Helen's phone went off. She could tell it was a text from the ringtone. She jumped about a foot and grabbed her phone. It was a message from Lilly, who was still trying to get together with her to let her know she and Ryan were an item.

"Are you upset with me or something? I've been trying to get together with you since last week, and you can't find an hour to meet with me?" Lilly asked.

She texted Lilly. "I'm sorry, Lill. I've had so much going on at work, which means some of the people I'm responsible for have been in crisis. Getting them through will make a difference for the rest of their lives. I want to see you. I will be in touch as soon as I'm out of the woods. I love you, and I miss seeing you."

The clock was ticking very slowly toward 6:00 p.m., and the office had almost cleared out as people headed toward dinner with their Valentines. They had notified the staff to stay home tonight if at all possible, telling them they'd received a warning from the police about possible violence but not relating it to the gang query they'd put out several weeks ago. They didn't want anything to get back to the gangs that might lead them to believe the police knew something was up.

At 6:15, the elevator dinged as it stopped at their floor. Maggie stepped off, looking like a million bucks in skinny jeans and high heels. She was serious for a change.

As she approached them, she said, "Joey didn't show up at LeBar, so nothing to report." Helen thought she was worried that her sleuthing days could be over, and she was clearly disappointed.

Maggie sat down with them, grabbed a piece of pizza, took a bite, and dropped it on the paper plate in front of her. "I love this pizza, but I just can't choke it down tonight," she said, listlessly.

She, too, began listening to the clock tick.

CHAPTER 42

Parker sat in a van that was tricked out with every state-of-the-art surveillance gadget money could buy. His and Frances's money, to be specific. He and several team members monitored the area for movement. They were staked out in the central freight yard, located right off Lake Shore Drive. There were two trains sitting on the tracks that had come in earlier. At 6:00 p.m. a third train had moved into the yard. So far, no vehicles had approached any of the train cars.

Another surveillance team was stationed in the storage yard where the intermodal containers were stacked after being unloaded and before being reloaded with a new shipment. They, too, watched for movement. Nothing so far.

In the meantime, SWAT teams were on the rooftops of buildings along Sheridan Road from Devon and to the north for several blocks. There were cameras on the storefronts of so many businesses these days that they were able to monitor activity on the ground by linking into the computers they fed into.

People moved up and down the street, in and out of

restaurants and stores, not knowing they were at great risk. Around 6:00 p.m., the proprietors of the establishments began asking patrons to wait inside, as they'd been warned there might be a disturbance on the street. At 6:15, people began to complain, and proprietors had to let them go if they insisted.

At 6:30, the first shot rang out, and people began to scatter. The shot was on a rooftop at the north end of the 1000 block of Sheridan Road. It was from the gun of an FBI SWAT team member who'd seen movement on the rooftop across the street. It was fortunate in that it helped to clear the street of pedestrians, but it wasn't clear whether he had intercepted potential shooters or mistakenly warned them.

And then all hell broke loose. Shots began to ring out from rooftops on both sides of the street. The gangs had split their snipers and stationed them on rooftops on both sides of the street, and FBI agents were struggling to identify the location of them all. They had checked out the roofs prior from the air, as well as on foot. The shooters had to have been in the building, having ready access to the building from a room within, or they could not have gotten to the rooftops so quickly undetected.

Regardless of the warnings and the gunfire, unwitting pedestrians moved about on the street below, and several were hit in the crossfire as gang snipers attempted to fulfill their contractual obligation of twenty-five to thirty casualties, while FBI agents attempted to intercept them.

It was all over in about five minutes. Several snipers were intercepted fleeing their posts, and others got away.

Ten pedestrians were shot that night. Two died. Three FBI agents were wounded, one mortally. Three gang snipers were taken into custody, none wounded or killed.

The gangs had succeeded in creating their diversion, but they had not achieved the number of casualties they had planned for and, as a result, had not created the crisis in numbers that would have drawn the first responders from all over the city.

News of the activity was on all media outlets almost immediately. First as an alleged incident, and then with witnesses on the street, and finally with interviews of the victims and videos from bystanders' phones. The mayor weighed in, taking a strong line against gang violence, "as I have throughout my tenure in this office, and as I will continue to do following the election."

Tom, Robert, Helen, and Maggie huddled around Helen's computer, watching coverage of the incident, expecting that something was about to happen over in the train yard as this incident was being reported.

Helen called the house to check in with Frances and the others. She knew they had to be worried sick. Donald answered the phone.

"Hi, Donald. It's Helen. How are you all holding up out there?"

"Oh, Helen. I'm so pleased it's you," Donald responded. "We're waiting it out, as I assume you are doing. It's not easy. I know Frances is distraught. She hasn't been near the kitchen for days."

"I'm sure she is. I can't wait for this to be over, and according to *our* plan, not theirs!" Helen responded.

"Would you like me to get her?" Donald asked.

"If you think she's up for a short chat," Helen replied.

"I believe it would be helpful for her. Let me get her," he said.

When Frances came to the phone, she sounded strained to Helen. "Oh, Helen, I am so happy to talk to you. Do you know anything?"

"I'm sure you know as much as I do at this point, unless you've heard anything from Parker. Have you heard anything from Parker?" Helen asked hopefully.

"No, dear, not yet," said Frances. "I feel like I can't wait a minute longer to hear from him, and then I feel as if I never want to hear from him."

"I understand," Helen said. "It really depends on the news he has.

"OK then. I'm sure you've seen the shooting news from the North Side," Helen continued. "I'm at the office with Maggie and my boss and his husband. We have been watching online as the news is reported. But we don't know anything beyond that. I guess that was the best we could have hoped for. Minimum casualties, some snipers apprehended. It's all horrible."

"It is horrible," Frances agreed. "Keep in touch, dear, and we will do the same."

"Will do," Helen replied, and the call ended.

CHAPTER 43

At the train yard, Parker and his teams listened to the news from the North Side, also expecting to see activity sometime soon. Parker checked in with his lieutenants around the yard, and they waited.

And they waited.

At around 9:30 p.m.—that is, three hours after the shooting on the North Side—a vehicle pulled into the yard. It was a small SUV. The vehicle circled the yard and left.

"Are you watching this?" the FBI agents staked outside the freight yard asked as they monitored the movement.

"We are," Parker replied. "It's on our scanner."

Thirty minutes later, a delivery truck pulled into the yard. It approached one of the standing trains, pulled beside it, and parked, turning off its headlights.

"And here we go," the agents said to the teams.

But nothing happened for the next seven hours.

At that point, the day workers began to arrive at work. It was 5:00 a.m., and the engineers were reporting to work. The mechanics were working on engines, intermodal containers were being stacked and unstacked, and the dock workers began to load and unload containers from truck to train car and from train car to truck.

Parker's vehicle was approached by a security guard who'd just come on shift. He banged on the driver's-side window. They decided to remain in the back of the vehicle, giving the impression, hopefully, that the vehicle was unoccupied.

They saw the security guard take out his cell phone and call into the office.

"There's a van parked in the freight yard. I have no paperwork. Is it authorized? If not, call the police."

Parker quickly contacted the detectives and had them deal with the call as it came in. He also asked that they handle the other vehicle as well, the one parked by the stacked box cars.

Parker alerted the vehicles parked outside the yard. These vehicles were to follow the shipments to their delivery points.

"The security personnel are checking vehicles. You guys should all be good, but I've asked the city people to let them know we're all authorized.

"Do we have any evidence of electronic communication from the yard to outside sources?" asked Parker of the FBI and detective teams.

"No. None," came back over his earpiece. "We've searched the airwaves for sophisticated communication devices but found none. This seems to be a true gang operation, meaning they had their orders and are moving through them. It's what makes them an excellent partner for this type of job. They know their stuff and require nothing in writing or over the airwaves."

Parker did suspect that the lower casualty count of the North Side diversion, which meant a smaller crisis, most likely gave Joey, or whomever, cause to rethink the plan.

"The lower impact of the diversion gives them less time to load, unload, and deliver their product," Parker said to his team. "And the SWAT teams on the roofs let them know their initial plan had been hacked to some extent. As a result, most likely, they are on to plan B, whatever that is.

"Either way, they have to deliver on this deal somehow. They're a fine-tuned operation, and if there are new orders from the top, the guys on the ground know what's expected of them. We're just going to need to observe and follow them."

As activity around the yard kicked into full motion for the day, there were trucks entering the yard and lining up around containers to empty them for delivery. This was going to be difficult.

Parker radioed the vehicle stationed by the stacked boxcar inventory to find out what was happening over there.

"Nothing," was the reply. So, everything was happening in the yard with the cars that had come in over the past twenty-four hours, and nothing was happening with the stored cars.

"Watch carefully," Parker said. "What's happening out here could very well be a diversion to keep our eyes out here and away from there."

At noon, the movement in the yard changed as workers began to break for lunch. Some headed to food trucks parked on the street outside the yard, while others found a place to sit and eat what they had brought with them.

"Keep an eye out," the FBI team said. "Things happen when people begin moving around."

CHAPTER 44

Helen had waited up the first night with Tom, Bob and Maggie, until, at dawn, they all agreed to go home for a break, which would include a shower, some clean clothes, and a nap. They'd keep in touch though.

Helen dropped Maggie at her rooming house. "Try to get some rest, Maggie. And you've done a great job with this situation. I'm so proud of you."

Maggie looked uncomfortable. She wasn't used to being praised, but she was too tired to think of something sarcastic to say, so she just nodded and looked away.

"I'll pick you up again at noon," Helen said. Maggie even agreed without arguing, very un-Maggie-like, and dragged her exhausted self upstairs and into the house.

Helen had barely made it up the stairs to her first-floor flat. It was Thursday morning, and her roommates were getting ready for work when she came in.

"Where've you been, wild thing?" one of them said, albeit half-heartedly and almost inaudibly between slurps of life-giving coffee.

"Working," Helen said as she moved toward her bedroom door.

"At least you weren't out on the street last night. Did you hear what happened up north?" Slurpy asked, almost inaudibly.

"I did," Helen said. She skipped the shower, set her alarm for 11:00, and fell into bed.

Maggie woke up at 10:00 a.m. She'd had four hours of unbroken sleep, in a warm bed, under clean sheets—in other words, a full night's rest compared to freezing under a bridge in filthy dirty clothes, with people screaming while mufflerless cars roared by. So, truly, a full night's rest.

She knew LeBar opened for lunch at eleven o'clock and thought she'd get herself cleaned up and head down there to chat up the bartender.

She Ubered downtown and perched herself on her normal barstool. The bartender, Gloria, was busy pouring wine for the ladies who lunched on the Mag Mile when Maggie casually asked, "Any sightings of my buddy?"

Gloria knew who she was talking about, having served her and Joey Caruso at the bar several times this past week. "Haven't seen him," Gloria replied.

And as if the universe had heard, she was amazed to see Joey himself plop down on the stool next to her. He looked like crap—much worse than she did, she noted proudly.

"You sick?" she asked innocently, taking a sip of her Coke. "You look like shit."

"Nope. Rough night though. Not much sleep," Joey replied. "And tonight won't be much better."

"Work?" she asked, again very innocently.

"Yep," he said, ordering a double shot of Jack. "I won't make it too long. Just stopped in for a sedative, and I'm off to bed."

"Good call," Maggie replied. She started to get up as though she had just stopped to have a Coke before picking up her carry-out lunch. "See you around."

"Yep," he said again. "Yep" and "Nope" were all the vocabulary he had at this moment it seemed.

Maggie grabbed a cab and headed back to her place just as Helen pulled up in front.

"Maggie!" Helen yelled. "Where have you been?"

"Can you get Parker on the phone?" Maggie asked, and Helen hit send.

"Parker? It's Helen. I'm with Maggie."

"Hi, Mr. Bennett," Maggie said, as though she were applying for a job. "I just saw Joey Caruso at LeBar. He said he'd been up all night and would be again tonight. I don't know what function he has as part of this, but I wanted you to know he's actively participating. Oh, and he was headed home, or somewhere, to sleep, so whatever is happening, it probably isn't happening during daylight today."

"Thank you, Maggie," Parker said. "That is really valuable intel."

Maggie smiled. She could tell Helen was proud.

Helen called Frances after they'd talked with Parker. She was still parked in front of Maggie's boardinghouse.

Donald answered, as usual.

"Hi, Donald," Helen said. "Holding it together out there?"

"We are, Helen. You?" he answered.

"Barely," Helen replied. "I'm with Maggie, my client who has been helping us with intel on this case. I've mentioned Maggie to Frances before. I'm wondering if we might head out to the house for a few hours. Based on information Maggie has gathered, it doesn't seem as though anything important will be going down this afternoon, and we're antsy."

"Just a minute. Let me get Frances," Donald said.

"Hello, Helen," Frances said when she came to the phone. "I am so happy to hear your voice, dear."

"And I am happy to hear yours," Helen responded.

"Donald says you and your friend Maggie were considering a drive out to see us. Please do come," Frances said. "It will give me a reason to go into the kitchen and bake something special, and I would be so grateful for a diversion. What time would you arrive?"

"I hope we can be there in an hour or so, depending upon traffic," Helen replied.

"Wonderful! Don't stop for lunch. We will gather at the table and console ourselves," Frances said. "Well, I must go prepare for company! See you both soon."

Maggie looked amazed. "I don't believe I've ever felt as welcome anywhere as I feel at this very moment," she said.

"Prepare to be amazed," Helen replied.

CHAPTER 45

Marty had spent another day in hell—a.k.a., the garage. Same thing. They had once again forcibly injected him with a solution of heroin, after which he'd been in a fog, his awareness severely compromised. By evening each day, he would be coming out of the fog, only to feel the pain of withdrawal and craving more heroin, something he'd planned never to feel again. He would be happy to see them when they came with the next injection.

The others in the garage continued to steer clear of him. They didn't want to interfere with whatever it was Sammy was doing with this guy.

Marty grabbed a bagel and went back to the mattress he'd been sleeping on, when one of the guys who'd just joined them in the garage announced there'd be activity tonight, and they'd be working, so now would be a good time to rest.

Those who had been with him for the past four days went to their mattresses. Those who had just joined them sat around the coffee pot, talking.

"I understand we'll be unloading heavy boxes, so that

means guns I think," the large man they called LeShawn said to another man. It appeared LeShawn was in charge here now, so he was probably the most knowledgeable about what would happen next.

"Sometime after midnight?" his counterpart asked.

"Right," LeShawn replied, after which they both stuck their heads in their phones, and no further intelligible dialogue could be heard by Marty.

Marty's goal at this point was to survive, but if he didn't, it would save him a lot of suffering. He now knew he could live a good life with people who cared about him. He also knew he had talent that others saw and valued. And he knew that getting back to it would be a long and arduous journey to recover from addiction. He'd taken that journey before and didn't relish the idea of going through it again. If he didn't have to go on that journey, that was fine too.

CHAPTER 46

Traffic was light that Thursday as Helen and Maggie pulled up to the house about fifteen minutes early.

Maggie's eyes kind of bugged out as she said, "OK, Helen. You've brought me somewhere to kill me and dump my body in a river?"

"Exactly," Helen said. She shut off Edith and told Maggie they had arrived at their destination.

"Right," Maggie said. "Like the last couple weeks haven't been weird enough. Let's go for lunch in an abandoned house in an area that reeks of exhaust fumes."

"Yes," Helen replied. "Let's."

Helen had learned to follow Frances's tracks and park in the back of the property to avoid the hundred-yard dash through rubble and overgrowth. She led Maggie to the back steps and said, "Watch your step," as she hopscotched from board to board.

Maggie followed, with great alacrity Helen noticed. Obviously not her first abandoned house. Knocking gently, the door swung open, and she was pulled inside by Frances, who hugged her as though she had thought she'd never see her again, followed by the same treatment for Maggie, whom Frances had never met before. Clearly Frances was strung out.

The smell of exhaust fumes, however, if a problem outside, was supplanted inside by the most wonderful scents.

Maggie stared in amazement as Frances greeted her effusively. "And you are Maggie. I've heard so many wonderful things about you, dear. You truly are an amazing young woman according to all accounts, and I am honored to meet you."

"You are?" Maggie stammered. "Well, thank you very much. And likewise."

"Helen knows the routine," Frances continued. "I'll be busy here for another forty-five minutes, and we'll eat at one thirty. We are having a late brunch buffet with beef tenderloin, Yorkshire pudding, eggs benedict, various bakery items that will be coming out of the oven shortly, and wonderful fresh ground coffee."

"Wow," Maggie said. "Wow."

"I thought a late breakfast would be good for you girls, given that you burned the midnight oil last night and are only just now starting the day."

"Right as usual," Helen responded. "We'll head into the living room so Maggie can meet everyone."

"Everyone?" Maggie's eyes said.

"Follow me, Mag," Helen said and headed toward a door leading out of the kitchen and into the dining room, where there was the most beautifully set table Maggie had ever seen.

Maggie was about to make a sarcastic remark about Martha Stewart being a resident but decided to just be quiet and take it all in. Helen had been right; she should have prepared herself to be amazed but had not. Hence, she was just going to have to be amazed with no preparation.

They proceeded through to the entryway, where there was a fountain, to Maggie's continuing wonder. They heard muffled voices as they proceeded toward the living room. Everyone stood up when Helen and Maggie entered the room, and Donald said, "Oh thank God! You came. We are so happy to have a break in this interminable waiting." The others agreed.

Helen introduced Maggie to Donald, Emma, Angela, and Zachary, asking them to share a bit about their work as Donald poured tea for Maggie and Helen. When it was Zachary's turn, Maggie could see he was struggling.

"Marty and I collaborate on music and lyrics," Zachary said. "He does the music, and I do the lyrics. We have had some unanticipated attention from very high-profile people lately and were just getting ready to enter into an agreement for even greater exposure. We are all worried sick about him. He is a talented and amazing person with the heart of a lion."

Now it was Maggie's turn, and Helen urged her to share something about herself.

"My name is Maggie Dax. I have been in and out of trouble since I was a young child. I've lived through numerous foster care situations, some where they were horrible to me and others where I was horrible to them. And I am now under Helen's supervision, although that will end next week I believe. Correct, Helen?"

"Yes," Helen answered. "But continue."

"I think that's about it. What more can I say?" Maggie asked.

"You can say that you have contributed information to the authorities and to Mr. Bennett throughout this ordeal by interfacing with gang members and even being arrested to follow an informant to jail. And most recently, you interfaced with the person who coordinates gang activities throughout the city and reported on his whereabouts, confirming their suspicions that information is being coordinated between gangs as this crime unfolds."

They all looked at Maggie with great fascination.

Donald said, "So, a brave young lady then."

"Yes," Helen responded. "A very brave young lady. Too brave, I sometimes think."

Maggie sat quietly. It was clear she had never heard herself described in these terms. Nor had she felt the admiration of people for whom she had admiration. It was messing with her mind a bit.

CHAPTER 47

"Bennett," Parker answered. One of the team members from the storage area was calling to report.

"There's movement on the tracks. Empty flatbeds are starting to roll into the area to collect containers to fill. Our scanning equipment shows that some of the empty boxcars have something in them. They are not full but have some remnant in them, perhaps of a past shipment or perhaps of illegal inventory, hidden for consolidation at the point of unloading."

"This," Parker responded, "may be what we've been waiting for."

Parker coordinated with his FBI counterparts and continued to watch as the cars were loaded onto empty flatbeds. This took four hours, after which the engine pulled the full-length freight train out into the open air of the yard. By the time the train had taken its place, it was the end of the day, and workers were leaving the yard.

As they continued to wait and watch, they began to see a curious set of movements. Team members radioed back and forth, reporting what they were seeing.

"Cargo trucks pulled up perpendicular to the doors of a few of the newly loaded boxcars. Doors to those cars are opened slightly, about five feet, and product is being unloaded from them," they reported.

By midnight, these trucks began to pull away from the yard, and the plan kicked into full gear. FBI and city agents followed as the trucks moved north, south, and straight west in the city.

Traffic was light, but the streets were by no means empty. The streets were never empty in a city of close to three million people.

The trucks proceeded in three different directions with satellite surveillance and vehicles tracking them from a distance, to remain anonymous. The first headed south on the Dan Ryan, exiting at Ninety-Fifth Street. It drove to Harlem Avenue, turned right, and made a sharp left into an alley, where it pulled in front of an old warehouse loading dock. By this time, the city detectives had been made aware of the route and took positions around the perimeter in anticipation of the cargo being unloaded into the warehouse to be picked up by customers. As the dock door opened and the back of the truck opened, the detective teams watched. Crates were unloaded.

They waited and watched for several hours. Eventually, as the warehouse lights were turned out and the delivery vehicle from the train yard pulled away, the city detectives decided to move in to inspect the shipment.

"Vegetables," the lead agent said in disgust. Specifically, carrots, onion, green peppers, and cabbage.

Parker had called Beverly as the caravan initially set out. "Hey, Beverly, I'm here at the train yard, watching a shipment being disbursed. I'm going to stay behind. If this is the real shipment, they can let me know, and I'll head out, but if these guys are as sophisticated as we have been led to believe, it could be a decoy shipment."

"That's great, Parker," Beverly replied. "I was thinking the same thing. If they know we had intel on the rooftop shooting, they'll figure we also have intel on the rest of their plan. A decoy move would absolutely be what I'd expect."

"OK, just wanted to let you know I'll be staying here," he said. "I'll be in touch if there's anything to report."

"Great. Thank you, Parker," Beverly replied, and the call ended.

After all vehicles had left the train yard, Parker quietly exited the van with two others, and they used the dark to move through the yard and into the building where the empty intermodal containers were being stored. There, they observed teams of men unloading boxes. The boxes were wooden, and they were heavy, taking two men per box to move. Three trucks were lined up at one dock in front of a container that was stacked at dock level among other containers. The men were moving fast.

Parker and his men returned to their van. He called Beverly.

"Well, it was a decoy. There are a bunch of guys loading the real crates now. They're moving pretty fast, hoping the diversion will keep everyone occupied for a while I imagine."

"Great, Parker. Great work. We're on it," Beverly replied, obviously excited that they might finally be dealing with the real thing.

It was not Parker's intention to interrupt this activity. His team would be fed intel on the location to the north in the hope that they'd find Marty. They sat quietly in their observation vehicle, waiting for the loading activity to conclude. Knowing the vehicles would be trailed from the exit to their destination by satellite allowed them to wait quietly without drawing attention to their presence in the yard or following too closely as they exited.

As the trucks began to pull out of the railyard, Parker directed his team.

"We'll wait fifteen minutes. I'll have the location from the FBI, and we'll head toward the location. Then we'll see what we find."

* * *

It was 4:00 a.m.

Moving up Twenty-Second Street, their vehicle entered the Circle Exchange, following it onto the Kennedy Expressway and exiting at Division. They were headed to Humboldt Park, where Maggie had attended the party and met her friend Tiffanie.

Humboldt Park was a beautiful, historic neighborhood, where tree-lined boulevards were bordered by mansions built by the wealthiest citizens of Chicago in the early 1900s. The area had, however, fallen victim to white flight, and for many years the beautiful homes became crack houses and refuges for squatters. It was just in the past ten years that gentrification had begun, so the area was transitional, and police spent a lot of time there trying to find persons of interest in various cases, because it was a good area in which to hide.

The truck turned into an alley and turned again into a large, old structure that had most likely been a stable a hundred years ago. The doors were pulled closed behind the truck, from the inside.

By this time, Parker and his team were out of their vehicle and moving around the area, grateful for the darkness, communicating quietly as they described the building and its access points to each other.

Parker said, "Guys, it looks like the west door will be the main access for business, since the others open directly into the garage. Anyone see a better access?"

Michelle, his team lead, said, "I'm stationed by that door. I don't see any other pedestrian entrance to the garage."

A short minute passed, and a truck turned into the alley, taking the team by surprise.

"Shit," Parker said. "These are either additional workers, or they are customers coming to pick up their product."

Again, they watched and waited. A short, stocky guy in a black knit cap pulled low over his forehead approached the west doorway, where Michelle was still watching. She was only about a foot from the man when he pushed the door open and walked in. He must have notified the guys inside by cell phone that he was coming; otherwise, he couldn't have just walked in without some serious fireworks.

Michelle said, "Well, how do you want to proceed? It could be that these various distributors are scheduled to pick up product throughout the night."

"Let's watch to see the interval between this customer's arrival and the next," Parker continued. "We'll wait the appropriate amount of time, and I'll go in at one of the regular intervals. You guys will need to apprehend and detain the actual customer when I do. Understood?"

"Got it, Chief," they replied.

They waited as the first customer exited, a truck pulled up, product was loaded into it, and the truck pulled away. This all took about thirty minutes. Parker thought he heard Marty's voice when the garage door was open, or maybe he just hoped it was Marty's voice.

Twenty minutes went by, and another individual approached the west-side door, pushed lightly, and let himself in. After ten minutes, a truck pulled up, and the individual who'd entered by the west door got into the truck as several guys who'd been in the back of the truck loaded wooden cases into it. The truck drove off, and the garage door closed. It had taken thirty minutes.

Parker wanted to get inside to check on Marty. He also wanted to let this parade go on as long as possible to crack open the whole operation. If they could disrupt this supply chain, their work would have far-reaching implications for organized crime countrywide. A lot of lives would be saved as well, since the product was obviously guns, most likely high-powered ones.

If Joey Caruso was as good as they imagined him to be, his organization would be tracking progress at all three sites.

The law enforcement groups at each site, and the satellite feed, were tracking vehicles as they were leaving each site, watching where they went and what they were doing with the product. A disruption at this site would be conveyed to the other sites, and they'd drop and run.

He decided to contact Beverly, the FBI lead, to discuss when he could go in to retrieve Marty with the least impact on the overall success of the operation.

"Hi, Beverly. We're watching a very interesting sequence of events here on the North Side. I want your opinion. I can integrate into the flow of customers going in to buy product and try to get my kid out. The question is, when do I do that? I don't want to diminish the impact of this OP.

"Does anyone know where Joey Caruso is?" Parker asked. "I can only assume from Maggie's intel that he is coordinating these activities and communicating across the city. When something goes down at one of the distribution sites, they will all know about it and shut down very quickly."

"We've had his apartment staked out for a week," Beverly said. "We haven't seen him come or go though, so he's not staying there now, and we know he hasn't been there for several days prior."

"What do you want me to do? I feel like Marty, the kid from Frances's house, has given the whole ten yards. He's risked everything. But at the same time, other lives have been lost in this operation. Those lives are just as important. I don't want to jeopardize the extent to which we all benefit from busting this whole thing wide open."

"Nor do I," Beverly replied. "Can you wait? I don't know how much supply they have or how many customers will come through the chain, but if you can wait, even an hour, at least we'll have that many more delivery trucks tracked and identified."

"Fair enough," Parker replied. "I will give it as long as I can. If things start to go wrong, we'll go in, of course. But right now, it seems like an orderly process, with fifty-minute intervals—thirty for business, twenty between customers."

"It will be dawn in two hours. If they're trying to wrap this up before it gets light, they have two hours to do that," Beverly noted. "Could you get a handle on how much product they were handling at the freight yard? And how much each truck is loading? "Beverly asked.

"This is a guess," Parker replied. "But it seems, from the size of the trucks that brought the freight here from the train yard, that the warehouse has about twenty-five crates. Each pickup takes five to ten of them. So they should almost be finished by dawn, which will take care of the darkness issue."

"So carefully orchestrated. These people are good. Thank you for staying in touch, Parker," Beverly said. "I am grateful for any amount of time you can give us."

"You're welcome," Parker replied, and cringed. He hated waiting.

⁕

Parker Bennett and his team waited another hour, watching this well-oiled machine operate. He was ready to go in and get Marty.

He called Beverly. "How's it looking at the other sites, Beverly?" Parker asked.

"Moving along," she responded. "Yours?"

"We've had three customers load trucks over the past two hours. I would guess we're getting to the last customer, Beverly. So maybe another hour, and they'll be finished," Parker replied.

"I think that's the consensus across the three zones. Would you be willing to split the difference and go in after this next customer, Parker? That will give us about as good an impact as we can hope to get."

"Yes. We've waited this long. I'll go in after the next shipment. We'll keep you posted," he said, and signed off.

"Everybody ready for this?" he asked his team. Michelle and the others responded. They observed the entry point for the trucks that were entering and exiting the alley. Michelle had the west door covered. And Parker was going to play it by ear when he got into the garage. He was uncertain how Marty would react when he identified himself. They had only talked on the phone. Parker hoped he wouldn't give him away.

They were uncertain as to the number of individuals in the garage, and each truck had a different number of individuals in it to load product. They assumed all, or many, were armed.

It was important to follow the rhythm of the previous four, soon to be five, pickups. Parker had asked the Chicago detectives for a nondescript truck to be parked on the nearest side street, with a driver to pull it to the garage door on cue. The bed of that truck had several armed agents inside. He and Marty would escape into that truck, or out a door, while federal agents entered through all locations simultaneously to apprehend the gang members working the shipment in the garage.

Parker contacted Beverly one last time before going in. "Hi, Beverly. I think we're ready here. Do you have a strategy for the other locations? Will you interrupt their pickups at the same time we interrupt them here?"

"What are you thinking, Parker?" she asked.

"The question is whether we can interrupt things here in such a way that they are unable to alert each other. And we can't really say before going in whether things will happen that way. I would think they have a fast communication tool at their disposal, if they're any good that is, and I think they must be good if they're working at this level," Parker answered.

"I'd let the other locations know we will be interrupting things on the North Side within the next half hour. That's what I'd do if I were coordinating things, Beverly. And the others can monitor the flow at the South and West Sides. If they see a change, they will know the operators have been notified to get out, and they can hopefully go in and apprehend them."

"I agree," Beverly said. "And I appreciate your experience and input, Parker. Be safe."

"Will do, Beverly. I appreciate working with you as well."

•᠄⫶ •

Parker Bennett approached the doorway as the actual buyer was silently apprehended by his teammates. They did not know the name of the man, but he was medium height and weight, a bit shorter than Parker and less in shape, but with winter clothes, it didn't matter. Parker also wore a knit stocking hat pulled low over his eyebrows, and his coat collar came up to his mouth, making his face somewhat hidden in case anyone in the garage knew this gentleman.

When Parker and Frances had talked about extracting Marty from this situation, Frances had never considered the possibility that Marty might want to stay. The drugs could have become a factor again, and there was also the possibility that Marty had chosen to go back to the gang. After all, that was what he chose last time he finished his period of supervision. Parker hoped Marty would be a willing participant. It would make it a lot easier to get him out if he was willing, presuming he was in the garage in the first place. If Marty didn't want to leave, Parker wasn't exactly sure what his next move would be. He'd have to think on his feet.

He knocked softly and entered the west door of the garage, as he had seen the previous clients do. In the small office, he was face-to-face with Marty. Another man stood across the room near the door to the garage area. Marty looked exhausted and not particularly focused. The other man was preoccupied as well, since it was Marty's job to ensure the money was wired to the offshore bank account. The other man was apparently the gatekeeper to the garage and the product.

"We take Venmo, or you can send a bank wire. Here is the account number. Please handle that immediately and in my sight. We will load the products after we have confirmation of the transfer," Marty said, with a voice that sounded electronically generated.

"Certainly, young man," Parker replied. Marty looked at him a bit strangely. His voice must have sounded familiar, but Marty wasn't immediately able to order his thoughts as to who Parker was.

While Parker fidgeted with his phone, the other man opened the door to the garage and walked through it, leaving it open. Parker said, "Marty, it's Parker Bennett. Are you ready to leave this place?"

"I have never been more ready to do anything, Mr. Bennett."

Parker smiled, although his mouth was still covered by the collar of his winter coat. He was ecstatic. The next step would be to get out of this place alive.

"Let them know my payment went through, and I will step outdoors. Follow me out the side door when the truck pulls up and they open the garage door," Parker said.

Marty looked stupefied. He shook his head and said, "Payment processed," and the guys in the garage listened for the truck to pull up, which it did as soon as Parker exited the west door and walked out to the alley, where he motioned to it.

The garage door opened. The truck bed door was raised, and the SWAT team was standing with weapons pointed. Others had entered the west door and had the gang guys loading the truck surrounded.

Marty had followed Parker through the west door as soon as the loading activities were initiated. Parker rushed him through the yard and to the street, where an unmarked car pulled up. They both got in. As they did, Marty said,

"They have me hooked on heroin again, Mr. Bennett. I swear I didn't take it voluntarily. They would inject me every night. I'm so sorry. I had no choice, believe me."

Parker said, "Marty, you will be treated by the best medicine has to offer. It's up to you now to get through this time, which is the hardest time, and then you'll be back at the house with your family and can go on with your life. We are all so relieved to get you out of there."

Parker instructed the driver to take Marty to Northwestern Hospital and keep him under armed guard. He was to be thoroughly examined and treated.

Returning to the alley, Parker asked the rest of the team if they had picked up any clues as to whether this group had had an opportunity to notify the west and south unloading points about the raid. They did not notice anything that would give them a clue one way or another.

He called Beverly as they dealt with the occupants of the garage and as he poked around to see exactly what was in the crates. The first one he pulled open was full of rocks, making it very heavy, just like a crate of guns would have been, but there were no guns. "What the fuck?" Parker uttered.

"It's a crime to unload landscaping materials now?" The guys being booked were now taunting the FBI agents who were detaining them. When they were processed for identification, it was found that all had prior offenses and were known members of North Side gangs, so there was no doubt that this diversion was intentional and part of a very well-orchestrated plan.

Beverly and Parker were both disgusted. They had been outsmarted twice. This operation had to be extremely professional and well resourced to have so many moving parts and to have outsmarted federal, state, and private agents with years and years of experience.

Now, however, they had the full attention of those law enforcement agencies, and it was time to play hardball.

"Let me call the other sites and tell them to go in. We'll find out if we have three sites with rocks. There may be one that is authentic and two that are not. I hope that is the case anyway. If not, there could be a fourth site or another day for delivery altogether. Shit!"

CHAPTER 48

"Yes, Frances, I was with him, and the few words we exchanged were about how thrilled he was to get out of there. He had not embraced the gang culture."

"Oh, thank God. When can I see him?"

"Well, Frannie, the problem is that he'll be in drug rehab, and there are restrictions on access for a period of time until patients are weaned from the drug and can get back to a healthy stasis," Parker responded.

"I understand," Frances replied, sounding relieved but not fully satisfied. She wanted to see for herself that Marty was in one piece.

"They forcibly injected him on a daily basis to keep a short leash on him. They also watched him twenty-four seven, so there was no way for him to go anywhere. He's beat this before, Frannie, without nearly the support he's got now. I know he can do it again. Have faith," Parker replied. He, too, was sickened by the idea that anyone would be forcibly injected with drugs to control them, but he was trying to sound encouraging and hopeful for Frances.

"I guess," Frances said. "I just hate it that he has to go through this again and that he is alone now."

"Believe me, Frances," Parker responded, "he is thrilled to be where he is. He's safe, and there's a light at the end of the tunnel. Before, it was only darkness."

"OK. Thank you, Parker. I will call Helen and tell the others. Thank you so much."

CHAPTER 49

The entourage on the South Side went in and found more rocks. But the West Side had a different experience. All three sites had about the same amount of traffic at the same interval; however, the trucks on the West Side were larger. And the perimeter was guarded much more heavily than it had been on the North or South Sides.

The site for the exchange was another old structure. It had no side door as the North Side garage had. All transactions were secured in the alley, including a search of the pickup vehicles and the people in them. The money was transferred at the door as the materials were being loaded.

At approximately 6:15 a.m., the FBI agents decided to go in for a look. They were staged as vagrants and service people, with some hidden on high porches of abandoned buildings. When the truck pulled away and the door closed, they knew they had twenty minutes until the next shipment; they used that time to get organized until the doors were opened again. It became apparent after thirty minutes that this shipment may have been the last one. They were packing up to move out. It was critical that the SWAT team move quickly and efficiently.

A huge crash resounded through the predawn silence as a truck broke through the old door of the barnlike structure that had probably been built in the early 1900s. It was fragile but made of heavy wood. The truck that crashed through it was heavier. This had presumably been the location for all three delivery points—south, north, and west—and taken in the money for all three sites as well, meaning that Marty's and the South Side wire transfers were being processed on the West Side by James Washington, the accountant. It would not be a surprise to find Joey Caruso in that truck. At least they hoped they would find him.

As the truck sped down the alleyway toward the street, vehicles pulled out of garages lining the alley in front and behind, blocking law enforcement vehicles. While many agents and police vehicles joined in the chase, some stayed to search the barn and do their best to figure out what had gone on in there all night.

They found empty crates filled with packing straw. They found food wrappers and mattresses. They found a hot plate. But they found no guns. The guns had either all been distributed to the various trucks that had come through the line over the past several hours, or they were in the vehicle being chased. If the former, those trucks had been stopped and searched, and guns had indeed been found. If there were more guns that had gone undelivered because of the bust of the fake distribution centers on the North and South Sides, they should be in the truck being chased.

Soon enough, it became apparent that while some of

the guns might be in the truck, others were certainly on the street. Gunfire began to fly at the law enforcement vehicles from all sides of the street, some of it from very high-powered rifles. Additional guns were firing from the vehicles being chased.

The lead agent ordered the others to shoot with intent, but it was just before dawn and easy for snipers to hide. And the truck was cruising down Central Avenue at about eighty miles per hour. When it crossed Madison Street, the vehicles blocking for it turned inward and came to a halt, impeding the pursuing vehicles, and then the large truck disappeared into the night.

The men in the side vehicles were taken into custody. Emergency vehicles were called for those who had sustained injuries. Now it was time for agents to book and interrogate and for the others to go home. It was early Friday morning, and all of this had begun on Wednesday.

CHAPTER 50

Marty's inpatient care had begun in February, and by May, he was back at the house, clean and healthy. The house seemed whole again, and the stress of the past several months was a distant memory.

Helen and Maggie had stayed in touch when Maggie's supervision ended. Maggie stayed at the boardinghouse and kept working at the fast-food restaurant. What the gang members who drove through didn't realize was that she was now one of Parker's most reliable agents. Her observation skills, raw courage, and understanding of urban environments allowed her to see things the others did not, and she was on call for anything related to gang or urban investigations. Parker had even flown her to Boston for a case, which elated her, since she'd never been on an airplane.

Elton John and Bernie Taupin had signed an agreement with Marty and Zachary to develop some songs for Elton's album showcasing new talent. And the other day when the phone rang, it was Tom Cruise, who had been in London making a film. He needed a music score for it. Bono, Bernie, and Elton had mentioned Zachary and Marty. Cruise was interested in having them write a few songs for his review. He'd give them the context of the movie so they had a theme to write around.

Emma had been hired as the understudy for Elphaba in a new production of *Wicked* that would begin in Chicago. They were rehearsing for six months and then would have a year's run, if all went as planned. And beyond that, they'd most likely travel to other cities, where she'd have a shot at the lead.

Poor Angela was still under lock and key while they watched the ever-menacing Rooney. He really was out of his league, given the sophistication of criminal activity in this city, but he was too stupid to know it. He'd get caught up in his own arrogance, her roommates encouraged her. Just a bit more patience.

Her consolation was that she and Zachary had formed a strong bond while Marty had been gone and Emma was out rehearsing. The others were so pleased. The couple had an easy and considerate dynamic between them. It seemed that just being around Frances made people kinder and more generous. It didn't hurt that there were really no threats in this home either. Outside, yes. Inside, no.

And there was another couple in the house as well.

It was 1:00 p.m. on a beautiful day in May. The trees in the unruly yard around the house were in full bloom. The ramshackle-looking windows would have been open to let in the scent of the blossoms but had to stay shut to block the noise from the highway and the exhaust fumes.

In the living room, the scents from a beautiful arch of red roses more than made up for it.

The residents at the house, plus Palmer, Helen, and Maggie, sat in chairs around the room, waiting. From the parlor came the sound of a beautiful, sweet, and calming melody, an original composition, composed by Marty for this exact moment.

When Marty finished the prelude, he rejoined the group. Zachary stood on the other side of the arch with a piece of paper. In front of him, Frances, looking like an angel in antique lace, with soft salt-and-pepper-colored curls draping down her back, stood with Donald.

Zachary began in his sonorous voice, "Dearly beloved, and I do mean that with all my heart, we are gathered here to share in the joy of a union that has been more than fifty years in the making. Today, Frances and Donald, our guiding lights, will pledge themselves to each other, with our support and love."

With that, he proceeded with a traditional marriage ceremony. He had obtained a license to marry online, but there would be no legal aspect to this ceremony. The pledge within this family would suffice to acknowledge the depth of love and commitment between these two people.

Following the ceremony, the celebration moved into the dining room, where the buffet and table had been filled with the most beautiful sweets any of them had ever seen, compliments of the incomparable Frances and with the aid of her new culinary assistant, Donald, who was wearing an elaborate apron that said, "Groom," on it.

The joy in the room was palpable. It was as much a

celebration of the love between these two people as it was the love within this family they'd created. Because it truly was of their own creation. They nurtured it, supported it, and basically loved it into existence, and they were proud of their family. As they said during the toasts, "You are the evidence of our love."

It had been quite a year at the house. Lives had been changed, and talents and abilities had emerged that the residents hadn't known they possessed. And it was only the beginning.

Printed in the United States
by Baker & Taylor Publisher Services